D0108306

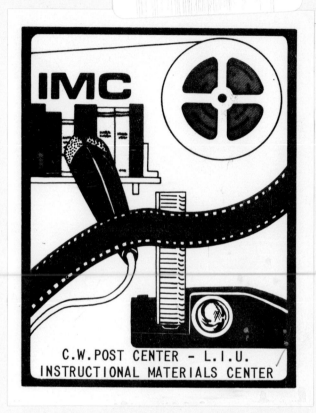
C.W. POST CENTER - L.I.U.
INSTRUCTIONAL MATERIALS CENTER

THE Visitors

Books by John Rowe Townsend

Top of the World

Noah's Castle

Forest of the Night

Written for Children

Modern Poetry

The Summer People

A Sense of Story

Good Night, Prof, Dear

The Intruder

Trouble in the Jungle
(originally *Gumble's Yard*)

Pirate's Island

Good-bye to the Jungle

THE Visitors

JOHN ROWE TOWNSEND

J. B. LIPPINCOTT COMPANY
PHILADELPHIA and NEW YORK

U.S. Library of Congress Cataloging in Publication Data

Townsend, John Rowe.
  The visitors.

  SUMMARY: Visitors from the future complicate the lives of several
inhabitants of Cambridge, England.
  [1. Space and time—Fiction] I. Title.
PZ7.T6637Vi3   [Fic]   77-7197
ISBN-0-397-31752-2

To Jill,

without whom, not.

one

There was this poet Coleridge, and one day he dozed off in his chair and woke up thinking he'd produced a master-piece in his sleep. All he needed was to get it down on paper. But he'd only written a bit of it when a person from Porlock came to see him on business and stayed for an hour. And by the time he was alone again, poor old Coleridge found he'd forgotten the rest. There was just a fragment of fifty-odd lines. You may know it. It's in all the poetry books. It's about Kubla Khan and the stately pleasure-dome that he ordered to be built in Xanadu. A fascinating poem, but frustrating, because there's no telling what was going to happen. That person from Porlock has a lot to answer for.

It's the nearest thing I can think of to my own experi-ence, but it's not really very close. It doesn't account for the pile of manuscript I found in my drawer recently. I'd have had to sleep for weeks and weeks to dream that much. And Coleridge at least knew he was writing his poem down; he didn't push a pen in his sleep. I have no clear recollection of writing the account that follows.

we had exams about to begin for which we needed to review. And Alan and I were asking each other questions out of the history book about President Wilson's fourteen points and the Treaty of Versailles and all that.

Actually we weren't getting on with it very well, because we were watching people fooling about on the river in punts and canoes. The standard of incompetence in boat handling on the River Cam, once the tourist season has started, is probably unrivaled by anything in the history of navigation. I had bet Alan ten pence that we would see somebody fall in before five o'clock. Now it was ten to five, and it looked as if I'd lose my money, because although boats kept colliding and people were slipping, tripping, overbalancing, shouting and squealing and generally making themselves look silly, nobody had actually fallen in, and the busiest time of day was past.

Then there was a spell of a minute or two when the river was suddenly empty and quiet, and we got back to our studies, and Alan started asking me about the Treaty of St. Germain. And *then,* from the same bank as ourselves but below the parapet of the bridge, there were voices, panicky and rather loud. And the panic wasn't like the pretended panic of people fooling around in boats. It was the tone of real, strong, sudden anxiety.

"Hold!" somebody shouted. It was a woman's voice, clear and commanding but tense. "Hold your breaths! And each other! Arms round! And don't move till I say you can. Ho-o-old! Now wait . . . Don't move yet . . . DON'T MOVE till I tell you . . ."

Alan and I had turned to look in the direction of the sound, but we couldn't see anything. There were no boats in sight and there was nobody on the bridge. But just

10

beside the bridge, on our bank, was a big beech tree, below which the ground sloped steeply to the river. Anyone under the tree at that point, though only a few feet away, would be hidden from us. And that was where the voices seemed to come from.

Silence now for a few seconds. Then a different female voice, quieter, contralto: "Sonia, is everything all right?"

The first voice again, reassuring but still with tense undertones: "Of course it's all right. I told you, Margaret, it's all routine. But keep holding and don't move."

Alan said to me in a baffled tone, "Hey, John, I feel dizzy!"

And so did I. Suddenly it was as if I'd just pirouetted in a dozen circles. The lawns and buildings of King's, the river, Clare College and bridge were moving round, swaying, tilting. Alan and I were sitting side by side on the bridge, yet now I could scarcely look into his face because we both seemed to be moving in relation to each other.

The first voice came again. The accent was one I couldn't quite place. "Right!" it said. "That's it. Here we are. Relax."

A male voice now: "Sonia! Has it happened? Has *anything* happened?"

"It's happened, all right!" There was relief in the first female voice, the clear, strident one.

The contralto voice said, "It's not *that* much routine, Sonia, is it?"

"Well, it *is* routine," the first voice said. "But it's always nice to know that nothing's gone wrong. That could be disconcerting."

The man's voice again: "Sonia, are you *sure* it's happened?"

11

The first female voice: "David, I assure you it's happened. Wait till somebody comes in sight. Or look up. Look up at the tree."

The second female voice: "Oh. Oh, yes, look at the tree!"

A punt came gliding through the bridge from the direction of Silver Street. The first voice went on, "And the boat. *Now* do you believe it's happened?"

The male voice: "But that's just a punt."

The first voice: "Yes, of course it's a punt. But look at the people in it. Their clothes."

The second female voice: "Yes, David, their clothes. That settles it."

A brief pause. Then, the male voice: "Can we unlink, Sonia?"

The first female voice: "Yes, David. But be careful, move very slowly at first. Everything's still unstable."

Then two voices, a male and a female together: "Katherine! Are you all right? Katherine!"

And a third female voice, younger-sounding and a little shaken: "Yes, I'm all right. At least, I think I am. Yes, of course I'm all right!"

Alan and I were staring at each other. I was dizzy, but not so much so as I'd been a minute earlier.

"What on earth goes on?" Alan said.

"Don't know. A radio play?"

Alan shook his head, impatient. "That's not radio, that's people. I'm going to see."

"Whatever it is," I said, "it's nothing to do with us."

I felt uneasy, though I couldn't have said why. But Alan was determined. He got up, then staggered.

"God, I'm still dizzy," he said. "Are *you* dizzy, John?"

"A bit."

The first voice came again, the commanding one: "Five minutes to seventeen. Call it five, remember. Check it on your watches. That's your watch, Katherine, on your wrist."

Alan, steadier now, walked round the end of the bridge, waved to me, and stepped down out of sight under the beech tree. I turned away, still anxious for some reason that I couldn't understand, and flipped over a page or two of the history book. I heard Alan say, "Good afternoon."

Then the first female voice: "Go back!"

Alan: "Why should I?" Alan is large, dark, and hefty. He looks like a football player, though actually he isn't one. Most of the time he's quiet, not aggressive at all; but there are some things that rub him the wrong way, and one of them is being ordered around. He doesn't like that. And when he's not liking something, Alan can be an awkward customer.

"I told you, go back!" The tone was brisk, sharp, and clear.

"Do you own this college?" Alan asked, in a quiet voice with an edge to it. Then, much more loudly, and with more astonishment than anger, "Take your hands off me!"

"You must go . . ." The commanding female voice trailed away. Then, in dismay, "Lost him!"

The second, contralto voice, anxiously: "What happened, Sonia?"

"We haven't got normal stability yet, that's all. He's gone."

too, but not of such striking appearance; he was fair-haired, fair-complexioned, round-faced, and amiable-looking.

The clothes of all three were quite ordinary. The man wore a tweed jacket, corduroy trousers, and suede shoes. The woman had on a pink shirt and a dark blue skirt and vest made of some silklike material. The girl wore a duffel coat and jeans. In spite of the ordinariness, there was something just a shade offbeat about the way they were dressed; their clothes were on the heavy side for a warm day, and all looked new. The man carried two suitcases and the woman and girl a soft-sided case each.

I still felt apprehensive about approaching them. But my anxiety about Alan outweighed my nervousness. I knew what I had to do. I planted myself in front of them so that they were practically forced to stop, and said, "Excuse me." And then I saw that they in turn looked apprehensive.

The man smiled and said, "Hello."

The woman smiled too and said, rather oddly, "Pleased to meet you."

The girl didn't smile and said nothing.

"I'm looking for my friend," I said. "I wonder if you've seen him."

At this I thought both the man and the woman looked positively alarmed, though they recovered quickly.

"He's a tall, well-built boy," I went on, "wearing a blue shirt."

"Tall?" the woman repeated, sounding surprised.

"Yes, he *was* rather tall, wasn't he?" the man said swiftly.

16

"You've seen him, then?" I asked.

The man and woman looked at each other. Then the man said reluctantly, "We did see a boy in a blue shirt just now, didn't we, Margaret?"

"I think we did," the woman said.

"Did you see which way he went?" I asked.

"I . . . didn't notice," the man said. He still sounded nervous. Then, less hesitantly, "No, I'm afraid we can't help you. Not at all."

He took the woman's arm, and all three moved away. To me they seemed a strange trio—tall, slightly over-dressed, carrying suitcases, and stepping out in a brisk, determined way. But nobody was taking any special notice of them. Cambridge in June is full of visitors of all kinds, and you'd have to do something pretty spectacular to attract any attention.

Were they foreigners? I didn't know. The accents I'd overheard from the bridge had sounded slightly odd: not American, not British, not quite like any I'd heard before, yet easy and natural enough. But when they addressed me the man and woman had spoken a carefully articulated standard English. They hadn't sounded foreign; they'd sounded more like amateur actors speaking in a way they'd learned quite well but weren't altogether comfort-able with.

Besides my puzzlement over the strangers, I still felt worried about Alan. I told myself it was unnecessary. Alan was well able to look after himself. But there was still no sign of him. I looked all round the beech tree and down by the side of the bridge, in case for some absurd reason he was hiding, but he wasn't there. Could he have fallen in the river? No, that was even more absurd. I hadn't heard a splash. And Alan was a first-rate swimmer; not that he'd have been in danger anyway if he'd fallen in, because the river wasn't deep. He'd have been back on the bank in no time.

The grassy space where the beech tree stood was bounded on one side by the river and on two other sides by an outlying building of King's College. It was just about possible for Alan to have gone into the building, though there was no reason why he should. Like most Cambridge buildings accommodating students, this one had several staircases onto which the students' rooms opened at various floor levels. I went to the foot of each staircase in turn and yelled "Alan! Alan!" as loudly as I could.

There was no response except for the opening of a first-floor window and the appearance of an irritated undergraduate face with the information, "No Alans around here."

The alarm I felt was growing. I wondered whether I should go to the police. But I would only make myself look silly if I did.

"A young man of seventeen *disappeared?*" they'd say. "Now then, be sensible. People don't vanish into thin air. Maybe he got fed up with you and cleared off. Or saw somebody he knew. Or remembered something he had to do. You say he was talking to mysterious strangers? Come now, you're not suggesting he was kidnapped, are you? Take it easy, son. He'll be home by bedtime. And anyway, it's not your worry, is it?"

Looking at it like that, it seemed obvious that there couldn't really be anything wrong. Yet I was still worried.

There was something very disquieting about the simultaneous appearance of the strangers and disappearance of Alan. And then I thought—yes, I'll follow them, see where they go, see what they're up to.

two

The strangers were still in sight. They'd walked round the edge of the great lawn that slopes down from King's to the river, and were about to disappear round the corner of the Fellows' Building. I sprinted after them. They didn't look round, and I was only a few yards behind them as they walked past King's College Chapel. This is the most beautiful building in England, according to some; but the strangers didn't give it a second glance. They moved as if they knew which way they were going. Their original brisk pace had slowed, however. The girl, in the middle, had taken an arm of each adult, and I had the impression that she was faltering a little.

They went out the front gate of King's, toward the street. I followed, a few seconds later, and thought at first that I'd lost them. Then I saw where they were. The girl was sitting on the low wall that bounded the college forecourt, a few yards from the street. She looked white-faced and sick. The man and woman, stooping over her, had their backs to me.

"My head!" I heard the girl say. "Oh, my head!"

I hung back, hesitating, wondering whether I could loiter around without being asked what I was up to; wondering in fact whether I wasn't being ridiculous and mightn't as well go straight home. Then the man turned round, and instantly recognized me.

Once again, just for a moment, there was an expression of alarm on his face. It was followed by a swift, friendly smile before he turned away from me and back to the girl, without saying anything.

On impulse I went up to them.

"Is she all right?" I asked.

The girl looked extremely miserable. She was hunched forward on the low wall, her arms tightly folded and her head well down toward her knees. The woman sat beside her and put an arm round her shoulders. Man and woman exchanged anxious glances. Then the woman said, in the same slow, carefully articulated voice as before, "It's not serious. Our daughter will soon be well."

The girl looked up and gave a wan, unconvincing smile.

"It's nothing," she said. "Nothing at all."

"It will pass," said the man. "She is . . ." He hesitated and went on. "Travel sick."

"We've come a long way," the woman said. She was looking at me directly, and now that I saw her at close range it struck me that she was extraordinarily beautiful: her eyes dark and deep, forehead high, expression both sympathetic and intelligent. The contralto voice was pleasant. She must be the one they'd addressed as Margaret. I knew the girl's name, too, from the conversation on the riverbank. She was Katherine, and the man, of course, was

David. I had the impression that the bond between the three of them was strong; and they were sharing a joint anxiety that nothing should seem amiss.

"We'd better not detain you," David said now. "I assure you, she will be all right soon."

This was rather more than a hint that I should move on, but I didn't feel like taking it. I was still intrigued, attracted, puzzled, worried, everything. Here were these three tall, rather strange people in the forecourt of King's, with their suitcases standing in a row on the cobbles beside them; and I wondered what on earth they were doing.

"Are you staying in Cambridge?" I asked.

"Yes. We shall be."

"At a hotel?" I cast a glance at the little pile of baggage.

"Yes."

"Is it far? Perhaps your daughter would be better if she could lie down for a while."

This was sheer impudence on my part, and they might well have told me to mind my own business. But I felt reckless, and in an odd kind of way I sensed that I was safely on the offensive. Both David and Margaret looked uneasy, even a little guilty.

"As a matter of fact," David said, "we haven't found a place yet."

"If you haven't made a reservation," I told him, "you may not get in at the big hotels. They're very busy at this time of year."

"I think we would not wish to be in one of the big hotels," he said. "Somewhere peaceful would suit us very well. Somewhere with privacy."

"What we need is rest and quiet," Margaret added.

It was then that I thought of Mrs. McGuinness. Mrs.

McGuinness used to come to our house as daily help, but gave it up when her husband was injured two or three years ago. She lives in a house near Jesus Green—actually it belongs to my father—and is a college landlady. With the academic year over, her student lodgers would have gone. Quite likely her rooms would be empty, and she'd be glad to rent them.

"I think I know a place," I said. "Nothing special, but quite nice and clean. How long will you be staying?"

"We might stay for some weeks," Margaret said.

David added hastily, "But we don't know. We haven't decided. Initially we only need rooms for a night or two, while we consider what to do next."

"Let me telephone Mrs. McGuinness," I said. "It won't take a minute. If her rooms are free, would you like me to bring a taxi round?"

Katherine, whose head had sunk toward her knees again, now looked up.

"A taxi!" she said. Her tone was surprised, as if I'd suggested a rickshaw.

"Yes, a taxi, Katherine!" David said sharply. "A hired automobile." But then he turned to me and said, "I don't think you should go to so much trouble for us. We are quite able to take care of ourselves."

"It's no trouble at all," I assured him. And before there was time for argument I left them, slipped across the street to a telephone booth, and called Mrs. McGuinness. And yes, she had all her rooms free and would be only too glad to rent them for as long as desired.

I returned to find my three people watching the traffic. Katherine, though still pale, seemed to be recovering slightly. King's Parade is a restricted traffic zone, so there weren't many vehicles going past, but the three were looking at everything with expressions of mixed interest and apprehension, and making remarks to each other which ceased as I approached.

"Yes, you can have the rooms," I said. I picked up two of the suitcases. "Let's just walk across to the cab stand in the marketplace. It's only a few yards."

They seemed to be hesitating.

"That's if you really want to," I said. "Don't let me push you into it."

"Oh, yes, yes," Margaret said, though her tone of voice struck me as doubtful. Then she smiled and said, "Thank you very much."

They stepped off the pavement with great caution, looking anxiously around them, and clearly uneasy until we got to the other side.

"Is this your first experience of our traffic?" I asked.

"Yes."

"It's very light here in King's Parade. Is it worse where you come from?"

There was no reply to that question.

"You're not English, are you?" I said.

"What makes you think that?" Katherine asked. "We . . ." But David hushed her.

"Actually," he said, "we *are* English, but we have been out of the country for a time." He didn't seem inclined to say anything more. And already we were at the taxi stand, where there was a cab waiting. I stowed the three of them into the back of it.

"I'll come with you, if I may," I said. "I haven't seen Mrs. McGuinness for weeks."

There was no objection to that. During the five-minute

journey the three strangers looked out of the cab window with great interest all the way, and I had the feeling that they were suppressing a constant urge to make comments to each other. Except perhaps for Margaret, none of them seemed greatly impressed by the sights of Cambridge, but they stared at the other traffic, at the pedestrians, and at the shop windows. At one point David burst out, ''That's a public house!''

"Yes," said Margaret. "An inn."

"It looks quite harmless, doesn't it?" David said. There was a hint of excitement in his voice.

"Of course it looks harmless," Margaret said, rather coldly. "The majority of such places *are* harmless." Glancing round, I thought I saw that her eyes were giving him a "shut up" signal.

"I shall *go* to one of those," David declared. "And have a drink." I thought I heard an intake of breath from the other two, but there was no comment.

Then David leaned forward to speak to me. "I'm a little out of touch," he said, "having just come back from abroad. But . . . er . . . I assume we pay the driver for this journey."

"Well, yes," I said.

"Will this be enough?" He took out a crisp new five-pound note. I noticed that he had a smart new leather wallet and that it was crammed with banknotes.

"Enough?" I said. "Five pounds? It's much more than enough."

"Even with a gratuity?"

"Tip," said Margaret.

"It's still much more than enough," I said. "You'll have to get change."

"May I ask you to deal with it for me?" David said. "I'm sure you know what to do." He smiled in an amiable, trusting way.

I was mildly surprised that a grown man should be reluctant to pay the cabdriver, but it wasn't the first or the biggest surprise I'd had that day.

"Yes, I'll deal with it," I said. After that, nobody spoke until we were in the street overlooking Jesus Green where Mrs. McGuinness lives.

"I'll have to introduce you to Mrs. McGuinness," I said. "What names shall I give her?"

"Wyatt," said David. This time there was no hesitation. "Professors Wyatt."

"We are both professors," Margaret added.

I wanted to ask "Where? What of?" but the taxi was drawing up outside Mrs. McGuinness's house. I paid the driver, gave David the change, which seemed to interest him greatly, helped with the baggage, and rang the bell. And having told little skinny Mrs. McGuinness who her guests were, I made my farewells at once.

"We're very grateful to you, er . . ." Margaret paused, obviously searching for my name.

"John," I said. "John Dunham."

"It's been good to meet you, John." She shook my hand.

"Perhaps we'll meet again," David said casually. "As for your friend, it's too bad you missed him, wherever he was. I hope he won't be annoyed with you for going off with us."

David sounded altogether more relaxed, as if he was losing the nervousness that all three had shown when I first spoke to them. And Katherine was looking better.

Her color was beginning to come back, and as she said "Good-bye" to me she smiled for the first time. I glimpsed again the resemblance to her mother. It was a nice smile, and suddenly I rather liked her.

"See you," I said. She smiled again, with slight puzzlement, as if she didn't know the phrase. I moved away.

As the door closed I heard Margaret say, "That was *not* a good beginning, David."

And I heard David reply cheerfully, "Oh, I don't know. It was all right. I expect I shall enjoy myself. I usually do."

three

I felt a strange, brief satisfaction at having got the Wyatts safely tucked away in Park Parade: a feeling that I might be needing them again and at least I knew where to find them. And this feeling was related to the anxiety I felt about Alan. As I walked away from Mrs. McGuinness's I tried to dismiss my own worries. All right, I told myself, so this trio had arrived and Alan had vanished without trace, all in the same moment. A curious coincidence, but it couldn't be anything more. I'd heard it said of me before now that I had a hyperactive imagination; well, this must be my imagination in the process of hyperacting. People didn't appear from nowhere or disappear to nowhere. The Wyatts had come from someplace and Alan had gone to someplace and that was that.

I headed back automatically toward the spot where I'd last seen Alan and first seen the visitors. By the time I was halfway there I'd almost convinced myself that nothing extraordinary had happened. I half expected to find Alan sitting calmly on the bridge as before, still studying his history book, looking up to ask me where I'd been, and giving me some perfectly simple explanation of why I'd lost contact with him.

But in fact I'd just turned into King's Parade when Alan positively reeled into my arms. He was as white as Katherine had been. I'd never seen him, or for that matter anyone else, so totally shaken.

"Oh, God, John," he said. "Tell me I'm not insane."

"Where the hell have you been?" I asked him.

"I don't know where I've been. I've had—I think I've had a hallucination. But so real. It felt like real, it still feels like real. John, I must be seven times round the bend."

"Come and have coffee," I said. We were just outside the Copper Kettle. I steered him inside and put him into a chair, and within a minute we had cups of coffee in front of us. Alan's hand was shaking, and a few drops spilled as he picked up the cup.

"On top of everything else," he said, "I'm dizzy. Things would go round in circles if I didn't stop them by willpower."

"You're not insane," I said. "You're in shock. Tell me what happened. Tell."

"You won't believe it," he said.

He dropped his head toward his knees, in a gesture rather like Katherine's when she was sitting on the wall. For a while he was silent. I wondered whether he was going to throw up, but he didn't. Eventually he picked up his cup again and succeeded in drinking some coffee.

"Do you believe in the supernatural, John?" he asked.

"No. Absolutely not."

"So if something happens that you can't find an explanation for . . ."

"Then you haven't enough information," I said. "Because if you had the information you'd be able to explain it. There has to be a rational explanation somewhere, or the whole of science comes to pieces in our hands."

"That's what I've always thought," Alan said. "So if you're faced with something that's totally unaccountable it's terrifying. Mind-blowing. It isn't just science, it's the whole world that comes to pieces in your hands."

"The most likely explanation," I said, "is that what you think happened *didn't* happen."

"Yes. Hallucination. That's what it has to be. But . . ."

"Come on, Alan," I said. "What's it all about? Give."

"Well . . ." He seemed still reluctant, still shaken. Then he said, "What did you think went on, down by the river a few minutes ago?"

"A few minutes ago? It was nearly an hour ago."

Alan looked at his watch, then back at me. There was fresh alarm in his face. "It is. But it can't be, it can't. Somebody's mad around here, and I've a dreadful feeling it's me. Go on, John, tell me what happened."

"Well. We were studying the Treaty of Versailles and all that, and we heard people talking under the tree, down by the side of the bridge. Curious stuff, sounding as if they'd just arrived and didn't quite know where they were."

"And we felt dizzy. At least, I did. I thought you said you did, too."

"Yes. But it passed off. And you went to see what was going on. I heard a woman's voice telling you to go back. There was a bit of argument, and then she said 'Lost him!' and it sounded as if she was referring to you. It was all rather weird. The others seemed worried, but she said

30

you'd be all right. I thought I'd better see what had happened to you, but I got dizzy again. And by the time I recovered, the people were walking away. But you weren't there. I couldn't find you anywhere. They said they'd seen you but didn't know where you'd gone."

"How many of these people were there?" Alan asked.

"Well, that's another funny thing. I thought I heard four voices, but I only saw three people. A man, a woman, and a teenage girl."

"There *were* four," Alan said. "There were two women, a man, and a girl. One of the women seemed to be in charge. The one who told me to go back."

"And what happened, Alan? For God's sake, *what happened?*"

"I didn't want to go back. She said it again. And then I got dizzy again, but much worse. Everything whirred round and round, faster and faster, spinning like a top, or like a whirlpool gone mad. And I was sucked into the middle of it, and then all went black."

"Like going under an anesthetic?"

"I don't know. I've never been under an anesthetic. Unless that was one. Perhaps it was. Because the next thing I remember, as if it was an instant later, I'd woken up. And John, listen, this is what scares me, it was *night.*"

"Night?"

"Yes, night. John, there hasn't been a night since I saw you, has there? It's still Friday, isn't it?"

"Of course it is."

"I don't know whether that's a relief or not. I *thought* it was night. I was in exactly the same place, but the people weren't there. And I was sick and dizzy. Horribly sick and

31

dizzy. I've never felt like that in all my life until today. I just sat, because I couldn't do anything else. And I thought already I was either ill or mad."

"And what did you think happened then?"

"Well, as I say, at first I just sat, feeling awful. And scared. It had gone from day to night in an instant, and the moon was shining, reflected in the water. After a while I got up, and I'd have gone onto the bridge, but there was a courting couple there and I didn't want to disturb them. I didn't look at them too closely. I mean, you don't stare at courting couples. So I went back to where I'd been, and that felt funny, too. There was something different about the tree, as if it wasn't the same kind or size. And I kept imagining there was a building on the other side of the river, where actually there are only gardens. A funny, curvy kind of thing, quite large, but only an outline, no lights. And I knew it wasn't there really, so I kept looking away and looking back again, hoping I'd stop seeing it, but it wouldn't go away. In fact, what with one thing and another, I was terrified."

Alan isn't the kind of person to be easily terrified. He isn't the kind of person to be carried away by imagination, either. In fact there are some who say he hasn't got any. But you could tell from the look in his eyes that he was positively living this story he was telling, and not liking it any better as he went on.

"And the next thing was, John, that I heard the voice of that woman, the one who'd been telling everybody what to do. She said, 'Found you at last. That's a relief. I was beginning to get worried.' And there she was, standing beside me."

"Alan, what was she wearing?"

32

"Oh, something quite ordinary. A plain summer dress, I think."

"You could see it?"

"I told you, it was moonlight. And I'd seen it already, before the dizzy spell; it was the same one. And then she faced me and took hold of my wrists. She was very strong. I started struggling, and she said, 'Don't worry, it's all right.' And then the dizziness came on, and I passed out again. And then it was daylight, and here I was."

"Alone and palely loitering, so to speak."

"Well, not exactly that. There were people walking on the paths and crossing the bridge, just as usual. But there was no sign of you, or any of the four we'd overheard, and nobody was taking any notice of me . . . And now you say it's an hour since you saw me?"

"Yes. Doesn't it feel like that to you?"

"No, it feels as if I passed out and came straight back. Except that things happened, or seemed to happen, in between. But that part of it doesn't feel like any given length of time at all. More like a dream, a very vivid dream. How long does a dream take?"

"A dream . . ." I said slowly. "Yes, it has to be. Not an ordinary dream, though. I reckon we hit on the truth a minute or two ago. Those people put you out with some kind of anesthetic. And I got a small dose, too, but I was farther away, so it only made me dizzy."

"I've never heard of an anesthetic that would work in the open air like that," Alan said. "And John, wait a minute. If that was nearly an hour ago, where have I been in the meantime?"

"Out cold, I suppose."

"Out cold? Here, on the Cambridge Backs? You tell

me I could lie unconscious for nearly an hour and nobody would take any notice?"

"They just thought you were asleep."

"Oh, come off it, John. What about *you?* Why didn't *you* see me?"

"All right, then, you staggered off somewhere, under the influence of whatever it was. And in due course you staggered back and woke up."

"Yes," said Alan slowly. "Yes, I suppose so. I have to believe that. What else can I believe that makes any kind of sense? But it doesn't feel like that to me."

"Listen," I said. "There's something very fishy going on. These people are up to something, and I'd like to know what it is. Though I must say, the ones I met didn't look like criminal types. They sounded a bit bewildered, out of their depth. Said they'd just arrived here, but they didn't say where from."

"You spoke to them, then?"

"Yes. To three of them. Not the woman you mentioned who talked as if she was running the show. I never saw her at all. But I spoke to the man and the other woman and the girl. They were quite odd in a way—their clothes and their accents and the things they said were all a bit offbeat. But then, you get all types in Cambridge in summer. I must admit, I rather liked them."

"If they are up to something, I wonder what it is."

"What do you have in mind, Alan? Terrorists from Ireland? Reds from under the bed?"

"Oh, I don't know. I'd like to get some light on this, though, just to prove to myself I'm sane."

"Come to supper at our house," I said, "and we'll get

some further opinions on your sanity. I must say you look to me to be as sane as you ever are."

Alan didn't respond to this mild ribbing.

"I don't know whether I want to talk to people about what happened," he said. "They really would think I'd been having delusions." He paused for a moment, then went on, "Anyway, I expect it's all over so far as we're concerned. We're not likely to see that lot again."

"I think we're *very* likely to see them again," I said. "At least, the three I spoke to. I know just where they are now. They're at Mrs. McGuinness's in Park Parade. That's where I left them, anyway. Of course, there could have been another disappearing act."

I made this last remark jokingly, but my grin became uneasy halfway through. Alan wasn't smiling at all.

four

When we got home, Laura had just come in from the garden with a big messy armful of flowers. She was sorting them out in the kitchen, untidily and absentmindedly, while she chatted with my older brother Ben.

Laura is my stepmother, though I find it hard to think of her as that. She's Father's second wife, and is just halfway between his age and Ben's. She isn't beautiful or even pretty; in fact she has a rather ugly, comic, monkey face, especially when she gives you her great big friendly grin. Laura is all right. She teaches at a local high school, and runs a biggish house without much help, and tries when she can to behave like a suitable wife for a successful man; so she's always behind the clock, with seventeen unfinished jobs on hand, but she doesn't let it worry her. Her real worry is over the health of her only child, my small half sister, Sarah. She doesn't say much about that.

Ben was at home on a visit from Bristol. He got a first-class honors degree in physics there last year and stayed on to do research, sharing an apartment with two friends. Like my father but unlike me, Ben is tall. He has a broad-browed, amiable face and brown eyes and very curly, very unruly hair, and wears big round spectacles. He has a relaxed, lazy way of talking, adapting himself to the level of the person he's with, so that a lot of people don't realize how clever he is.

I asked Laura whether Alan could stay to supper.

"He not only *can,*" said Laura. "He *must.* If he'll pardon me for giving an order."

"A special request," said Ben. "Not to say commandment."

"Your father's at home," Laura told me. "And the man from the Sunday paper."

"Oh, Lord," I said. "I'd forgotten about *him.*"

The master of Father's college—one of the most prestigious of the twenty-odd colleges that make up the University of Cambridge—was due to retire in a few months' time, and a heavyweight Sunday newspaper had interested itself in the succession and approached some of the possible candidates, asking for interviews. Father was one of these. He was telling everybody outside the family that he didn't want the mastership. Actually he wanted it like hell, and though he didn't altogether trust the press he thought he might emerge better from publicity than his rivals.

"So the family is on parade," said Ben. "A conversational supper. Special model for influential outsiders. Start polishing your witticisms."

"Oh, *Ben!*" Laura said, half-amused, half-exasperated. "It'll only be fish pie and gossip."

"In the Dunham household," Ben said, in the tones of one quoting from an article, "family meals are a free-for-all. Friends of the young Dunhams can and do drop in without notice. Hugh Dunham talks to them all as equals, on the topics that specially interest them. 'I learn from them continually,' he says. 'And perhaps they learn just a little from me.' "

"Stop it, Ben!"

"Well, he did say he'd be glad if somebody dropped in today, didn't he?"

"Yes, he did," Laura said. "He *likes* your friends to come. And here's Alan, so everyone should be satisfied."

"Your trouble, Laura," said Ben, "is an excess of loyalty."

"And yours, Ben," said Laura, "is an excess of cynicism."

"Much less dangerous," said Ben. But Laura had turned her attention to Alan.

"Alan!" she said. "Are you all right? You look a bit shaky to me."

"He's had a shock," I told her.

"Why, what happened?"

"Nothing, Mrs. Dunham, nothing," Alan said. He was obviously embarrassed. "I had a dizzy spell, that's all. It was over in a minute."

"You shouldn't have dizzy spells at your age," Laura said. She was concerned. "Have you had them before?"

"No, never."

"I don't like the sound of it. I think you should mention it to your parents."

"But Alan!" I protested. "Tell them what happened!"

Alan looked even more embarrassed.

"Nothing happened," he said.

Laura frowned, and exchanged puzzled looks with Ben. But Laura always has more things on her mind than she has time to worry about, and it can't be easy for her to find room for any more.

"I think you should get out of this hot kitchen," she said. "You'll feel better outside. Go and talk to Hugh and the newspaperman."

We went into the garden. Ben stayed in the kitchen with Laura.

Our garden is quite something. It's not large, but it's not small either. It's on the riverbank, it's sunny in parts and it's beautifully shady in parts. There's a fair expanse of grass and there's a rather fine copper beech tree. People come past in boats and point at anybody who's sitting outside, and you can hear their envious remarks. Father likes that, though he's inclined to be apologetic to guests about the fact that the place is obviously worth a small fortune. "We bought it when things were cheap," he tells people.

The house itself is a hundred and fifty years old, foursquare and plain and spacious. On the lawn there's a teak table, and this evening there was a tray on the table, with bottles and glasses. My father and another man and my small sister Sarah were sitting together, talking.

Father got up when Alan and I approached, and strode toward us, radiating affability. In spite of this, I had some doubt whether he would remember Alan's name. His interest in young people was somewhat intermittent. But he did remember.

"Hello, Alan!" he said. "Good to see you again. You're staying to supper, I hope? Fine. This is Terry Foster, from the Witness page in the Sunday paper. He usually writes articles about complicated, fascinating people in complicated, fascinating situations, but this week he's having a temporary lapse and merely writing about a handful of dry old dons. I'm one of them. Terry, here are my son John and his friend Alan.''

Terry Foster said ''Hello'' without getting up. He was small, thin, sandy-haired, and not terribly old—about thirty, I'd have guessed. He tilted his chair back, looking very much at ease. Alan and I said ''Hello'' in turn and then were silent.

''Terry was at the other place, I'm afraid,'' Father said, meaning Oxford. ''But he's really quite civilized. I'm sorry to say you've missed the photographer. He did his thing and went. Since then, Terry and I have had an interesting literary discussion with Sarah.''

Sarah, who is nine, had sat demurely with hands folded on lap while the introductions took place. She has dark hair cut in bangs, big dark eyes, and a small pointed chin. She's a rather solitary, self-contained child. Last year she was found to have a serious blood disease, but since treatment with drugs she's been normal, with no sign of illness. Apparently this is a remission—an interval after which the disease could come back. She doesn't know this. At least, she's supposed not to know it. I sometimes wonder what Sarah does know. She's a child who spends a lot of time with her own thoughts, and they may be more profound thoughts than people realize.

''We were talking,'' Father said, ''about Mole and Rat and Toad. It seems that Sarah finds Mole the most sympathetic, while Terry's favorite is Rat. Most enlightening. Myself, I must confess to a sneaking sympathy for Toad . . . Do you have views on Mole, Rat, and Toad, Alan?''

''Never heard of them,'' said Alan dourly.

I didn't believe that. Alan's family come from the industrial North, and he is inclined to claim an underprivileged childhood. Actually he does have trouble with narrow and uncomprehending parents, but he's never been all *that* underprivileged.

"They are from a very well known book called *The Wind in the Willows*," Father said.

"I *have* heard of that," Alan said. "But it wasn't part of my background."

"Oh?" said Father. I could feel him gearing up to interrogate Alan, with a view to convicting him of inverse snobbery. Apparently amiable but in fact extremely ruthless cross-examination was one of Father's techniques, and he practiced it with great, if showy, skill. But I didn't want him to practice it on Alan, who was apt to resent it and to grow sullen and sometimes rude. Besides, I still wanted to talk about our encounter.

"We had a funny experience on the Backs this afternoon," I said.

"I'm surprised that Alan goes on the Backs," said Father, "since I assume they were not part of his background." He was still hankering after a verbal conflict in which he would score graceful hits.

I went on rapidly, trying not to give him the chance. "A group of people suddenly appeared from nowhere," I said. "And Alan went to see what was going on, and *he* suddenly vanished."

"How strange," said Father. He sipped his drink. Terry Foster, eyes half-closed, tilted his chair a little farther back.

"Alan doesn't know what happened," I went on. "He felt dizzy, then he thought he was in the same place at

41

night, and that somebody came and fetched him back into daytime."

"Curious," said Father. But there wasn't any curiosity in his voice. I was irritated.

"This is something serious," I said. "It really *shook* Alan."

Nobody else said a word.

"Oh, go on, Alan," I exhorted him. "Tell them how it seemed to you."

But Alan looked embarrassed, just as when he'd been talking to Laura and Ben a little earlier.

"Drop it, John!" he said. "It wasn't anything, really."

"If Alan vanished," my father said, "I daresay it was for his own good reasons. Perhaps he got tired of the company he was in—namely, yours, John—and took himself off for a while. The rest of the story, no doubt, was just a leg-pull. Am I right, Alan?"

"Well, sort of," said Alan. "I really don't want to talk about it."

"Understandably," said Father.

"But listen," I said to Alan crossly. "Say what you like, you did disappear, and these people appeared, when there wasn't anywhere to disappear to or appear from. And they were such strange people—so tall, and carrying baggage, as if they'd just arrived from somewhere. I mean, you might expect people to be carrying bags if they were at the railway station or a hotel or some such place, but why should they carry bags along the Backs?"

"A profoundly uninteresting question," said my father.

"The people were interesting, though," I said. "They were tall, and two of them were dark, with kind of gold

42

complexions, very good-looking. And they spoke with different accents among themselves from when they were talking to me. They spoke in a slow, careful kind of way to me, as if they were practicing something they'd learned."

Terry Foster, who hadn't said a word or shown any sign that he was listening, now tilted his chair back into a normal position.

"They were tall, you said? And two of them good-looking and dark-complexioned? And seeming as if they'd just arrived that instant from heaven knows where?"

His voice was casual, but I could detect that there was interest in it.

"Yes," I said. "That sums it up."

"And I gather they spoke to you?"

"Yes."

"What about?"

"Oh, only about somewhere to stay."

"Are they staying in Cambridge?"

"Yes."

"You don't by any chance know where they are now?"

It was on the tip of my tongue to say "Yes, they're at Mrs. McGuinness's." And then something stopped me and I found myself saying "How should *I* know?" I can't really account for this. Perhaps it was because I had a sudden protective feeling toward the strangers and didn't want to discuss them with the man from the Sunday paper.

"Why do you ask?" I inquired.

"Why shouldn't he ask?" my father said. "It's a newshound's business to ask questions, and Terry is a newshound, though you mightn't think it to look at him. I suppose he's always on the trail of something. Not that I would have thought this was a particularly exciting trail to be on. But then, neither would I have thought *I* was a particularly exciting person to interview."

I had the impression all the same that Father thought himself considerably more interesting than the strangers.

Terry tilted his chair back again.

"Something that happened somewhere else made me start putting two and two together," he said, answering my question. His tone was lazy. "But probably I was making five. However, if you see any of those people again, either of you, give me a ring at the paper. And if you can get into conversation, try to find out where they're staying. I might be professionally interested. I'm not saying I *would* be, but I might."

"There are people of every size, shape, color, and accent in Cambridge," my father said, "especially at this time of year. The unusual is usual, you might say. I admit to a certain lack of interest in the dark strangers. Let's talk about Mole and Toad instead."

"Yes, let's," said Alan, anxious for a change of subject.

Father looked at him quizzically.

"The characters you've never heard of," he said, brightening. "Or so you would have us believe." He looked ready again for argument. But just then Ben appeared to call us in for supper. Glasses were picked up and people straggled inside. I was the last to go in, except for Sarah, who had listened quietly to the conversation. She took my hand.

"I think something funny has happened," she said. "Especially to Alan. I can sort of feel it reflecting back from him. He's scared, isn't he?"

Sarah makes strange remarks for a nine-year-old, and

has strange perceptions. I remember that for a day or two before Granny Holdsworth died Sarah was in a state of panic, and once cried out, "Don't, Granny, don't!" What makes it odd is that Granny Holdsworth wasn't ill or in any known danger. She stepped into the road in front of a heavy truck and was killed outright. Once it had happened, Sarah was perfectly calm. Father and Laura knew about this, of course, but put it down to coincidence. So did I. All the same, I treated Sarah's sayings with respect.

"I don't think he's scared, minnow," I said. "It's just that there's something he can't understand, and he'd rather not talk about it."

"I think he's frightened," she said. "And so are you, just a bit, aren't you? And it's to do with those people."

Ben came out to hurry us on.

"Let's get the supper seminar started," he said. "The sooner it begins, the sooner it'll be over. Come along, John, we're expected to sparkle. Though not so brightly as Father."

five

"Well, back to normal today," Laura said at breakfast. "Except for Ben being here. That's nicer than normal."

"Ben being here *is* normal," Ben said. "At least, it's normal sometimes."

"How long will you be with us this time?" I asked him.

"Only until he hears the call of the lab," Laura said wryly, "and that won't be long."

"Well, I'd better break it to you," said Ben. "There are a lot of things I should be getting on with at Bristol. I'll have to go back on Monday."

Laura made a face and changed the subject. "I thought everything went quite well yesterday evening, didn't you?" she said.

"Oh, yes. The great man was duly seen in his family context. As fascinating at home as he is in the lecture hall or on television."

"Ben . . ." Laura said in mild protest.

"And the great man's attractive wife, to whom he obviously owes so much. Elegant, petite Laura Dunham, the most charming of hostesses . . ."

"Ben!" Laura protested again, though she was laughing and not really seeming to mind. "For one thing, I am not elegant, and I'd say I'm little rather than petite. For another, that's the style of a women's weekly, not of Terry Foster or his highbrow Sunday paper."

"Let me finish," Ben said. "I've still to mention the great man's attractive children, the great man's attractive house, the great man's attractive garden . . ."

"Oh, shut up, Ben!" Laura said loudly, and he did.

Sparring between Laura and Ben goes on all the time he's at home. Actually of course she's very fond of him. In fact we are all fond of Ben, even Father, who tends to be absorbed in his own occupations. I used to hero-worship Ben when I was a small boy, and Sarah adores him in the same way. To her he's the ideal older brother—endlessly kind and patient, and perhaps even more so since her illness.

For a while there was silence, apart from requests for butter or marmalade. Breakfast in our house is a do-it-yourself, kitchen-table affair. This particular morning, only Laura, Ben, Sarah, and I were there. Terry Foster had left just after midnight, and this morning Father himself had been up and away early. He'd flown to a weekend conference in Paris. There was nothing unusual about that. Globe-trotting is part of Father's way of life. Going to bed late and getting up early don't bother him.

"Well, what's everybody doing, this fine Saturday?" Laura asked.

"I," said Ben, "am going to begin by clearing up all the debris from last night's meal. You're tired, Laura."

"Oh, no, I'm not," said Laura.

"Oh, yes, you are. Teaching all week, and looking after

Sarah and the house, and entertaining the Witness page into the bargain. Of *course* you're tired. You're going to leave this lot to me and relax with the newspapers. And next week you're going to try again to get a new Mrs. McGuinness to help you in the house."

"I've been trying for a year to find a new Mrs. McGuinness," Laura said, "and only got a couple of duds I was glad to be rid of."

Mention of Mrs. McGuinness switched my thoughts at once to the strangers. I told Laura and Ben what I'd said last night while they were preparing the supper. "And," I finished, "Father wasn't very interested in these people, but Terry Foster was. He sat up with quite a jerk."

"He was hungry to know," said Sarah, in a small, solemn voice. She had been eating cornflakes in a silent, self-contained way, taking no part in the conversation.

"He was more interested than he was allowing to show," I said thoughtfully. "And before he left, while Father was fetching his coat, he mentioned them again to Alan and me. Said if we could help his paper to make contact with them he'd be very grateful. I thought for a moment he was going to offer us money, but he didn't. All the same, I got the impression they might pay for information."

"Didn't you ask him *why* he was interested?" said Ben.

"Of course I did. He wouldn't say."

"No, I suppose he wouldn't. However . . . do you think your strangers might be up to something that would interest the Witness page?"

"I don't know. I don't read the Witness page."

"Well, it seems to consist mainly of exposures of

large-scale fraud, industrial espionage, and skulduggery of every description."

"Oh?" said Laura. "Which of those headings does the choice of a master for your father's college come under?"

"Academic skulduggery," said Ben promptly; and then, grinning, "No, I think it's just a bit of light relief for them, though I wouldn't be surprised if they managed to find a little gentlemanly intrigue going on. But mostly the Witness people go in for hard investigatory journalism."

"I can't believe the people I met are involved in anything sinister," I said. "They just aren't the type. They struck me as—well, rather innocent. Anyway, unless they've decamped they're staying at Mrs. McGuinness's."

"I gather you didn't tell Terry Foster that."

"No. I thought it would scare them stiff to have the press after them. *Should* I have told him?"

"No reason that I can see," said Ben. "I don't think *I* would have."

"That's good enough for me," I said. "I'll go on not telling him. I think I might walk across to Mrs. McGuinness's and see them this morning, however."

"Why not?" said Ben.

It was one of those clear blue Cambridge mornings when the approach across the Fen and along the Backs— wide and watery, open and peaceful—seems to clear the everyday junk out of your mind, open your eyes, refresh your spirits. Without actually deciding to do so, I found I was heading for King's Bridge. It was still quite early, there weren't many people about, and the corner by the beech tree was empty and harmless: no sense of mystery

49

about it, no atmosphere. King's College Chapel, more like lace than stone, looked as though it might float away into the sky any moment. It was fine and it was June, and I realized with mild surprise that I was looking forward to seeing the visitors again.

I'll admit that one reason for this was that I was interested in the girl. Katherine. It was an odd kind of attraction. She wasn't pretty, exactly, though you could certainly have called her handsome. Physically, the striking thing about her was that she was *perfect*. Her complexion, for instance. Not a trace of a spot or blemish. The whites of her eyes were the clear bluey-white that you sometimes find in children. Her teeth were flawless, her features regular, her figure just what it should be.

Yet it wasn't this perfection that turned me on. In fact it seemed, in some obscure way, to set her at a distance. And most of the time I'd been in her company, she'd had very little to say and hadn't shown any special interest in me. It was just her smile in the last minute before I left them all at Mrs. McGuinness's, breaking through at last after she'd obviously been feeling sick and ill at ease, that had appealed to me. I'd had a strong sense that contact could be made with this girl, that there was something very likeable there, if only I could find the right key.

When I got to the house in Park Parade, overlooking Jesus Green, it was to see the skinny rear quarters of little thin Mrs. McGuinness protruding from the front door. She was scrubbing the hallway just inside. She straightened up as I approached.

"They're still here, then?" I said.

"Oh, yes, they're here. Thank you for sending them. I can do with the money."

"They're paying you well enough?"

"Yes, they paid what I asked and no quibble. I could have asked a lot more and got it. Professor Wyatt gave me two weeks' rent in advance. You should have seen the walletful of notes he took it from."

"I've seen it."

"Gentlemen don't usually carry that amount of cash around with them these days. They pay by check or credit card or some such."

"I expect, being tourists, they don't have a bank account here."

"But they're not tourists, are they, John? They're university people."

"I suppose so," I said, "but they may be here as tourists. It's not the time of year for visiting academics. Anyway, what does it matter, so long as they're paying you?"

"They're a funny lot," Mrs. McGuinness said. "They don't seem to know what to *expect*, if you know what I mean."

I did know what she meant. It was just how I'd felt in bringing them across to her the previous day.

"Anyway," she said, "why don't you go in and see them? They have all my upstairs rooms. The sitting room's at the front."

I tapped at the sitting room door, and was told to come in. The Wyatts must have expected Mrs. McGuinness, for they were clearly startled to see me. They were sitting at a table studying what appeared to be three identical sheaves of paper. When I went in, the two older people, David and Margaret, jumped up, looking slightly guilty.

"Your friend!" Margaret exclaimed. "Is he all right?"

51

"Yes, he's all right. I met him on the way home, after I left you yesterday. He'd been feeling sick for a while, but he's none the worse."

"I'm glad of that," she said. I felt she was damping down her response, trying not to sound too relieved.

"He had a very odd experience, though," I said.

"Had he?" The apprehensive look I'd seen in her eyes the previous day was there again. I was sure she didn't want to discuss Alan's experience and would disclaim all knowledge of it. There was no point in pressing her. I let the subject drop.

"I hope you don't mind that I looked in," I said. "I just wondered if you were all right here. I feel a bit of responsibility, since I recommended the place to you."

Margaret smiled, relaxing at once. She and David had both sat down again at the table, but I noticed that all three of the little sheaves of paper had been pushed to the far end of the table, away from me. "It was nice of you to come," she said. "And yes, I think we shall like it. Mrs. McGuinness is very pleasant and helpful."

"We weren't bitten by a single insect during the night," said David cheerfully.

"David!" said Margaret. "Of course we weren't! One wouldn't expect to be bitten by insects in a respectable rooming house in twentieth-century England."

"I was joking," said David, somewhat abashed.

"My father's an enthusiast for the bad old days," said Katherine. "Mother's interest in old Cambridge is more architectural."

"Old days?" I said. "Old Cambridge?"

"It's an ancient and fascinating city," Margaret said. She looked embarrassed and slightly put out.

I thought I'd better come to the rescue. "It's a lovely day," I said. "Just the weather for seeing Cambridge, in fact."

"Yes, indeed," Margaret said.

"Perhaps I could show you round," I offered.

"It's very kind of you," David said quickly. "But I'm afraid we have a great deal to do. Unpacking, and so on. And some business. And, Margaret, I think you said we must go out and buy some things."

"Yes," said Margaret. She didn't sound enthusiastic about that. Then she said brightly, "But we can manage without Katherine. Perhaps *she* would like John to show her the city."

Margaret and Katherine exchanged looks. I wasn't sure that Katherine was pleased. But she looked at me and said, just a shade reluctantly, "Thank you, I'd like that. If it's all right."

Her smile came afterward, a second too late. Still, this was what I'd been hoping for. In five minutes' time we were walking together out of Mrs. McGuinness's house. I felt pleased about it. I didn't in the least mind spending a morning in the company of this tall, rather striking girl. I hoped we would meet some of my school acquaintances. They would be suitably impressed.

I meant to impress *her*, too. I knew what I would start by doing.

"If it's all right with you," I said, "I shall take you along the Backs in a punt. The Backs are where I met you yesterday."

"That sounds nice," she said. The smile came again. It was an odd smile, a social smile almost, a smile that had been remembered and switched on. Not like the one good smile I'd had from her the previous evening. There wasn't really any expression behind this one.

"I shall feel quite at home," she added.

"Oh," I said. "Do you have that sort of thing where you come from?"

I was sure she bit her lip. She hesitated for a second. Then she said, "Well, I like boats."

"Where *do* you come from, Katherine?"

It was the direct question at last, and she hesitated again before answering. Then she said, "We are from Jamaica. My parents both teach at the University of the West Indies, at Mona, just outside Kingston."

"Oh. I suppose it must be very beautiful there."

"Yes."

There was a silence that began to get awkward before she went on, "It's a beautiful island. Especially the north coast, between Port Antonio and Montego Bay. A great many tourists go there. It's almost as popular in winter as Florida."

Her tone of voice was flat and unenthusiastic. The thought crossed my mind that she sounded rather like a guidebook. There was another silence.

"And I expect you have plenty of friends there," I said.

"Yes."

Silence again.

"What do your parents teach?"

"My father history, my mother English."

"And are they going to be visiting professors, or something like that, in Cambridge?"

"No. We're only here on vacation. David—my father—has been here before, long ago. He wanted to come back. He thought my mother and I would like it."

"And do you?"

"Oh, yes, of course. What we've seen so far."

Katherine looked, in a curious kind of way, harried. She wasn't enjoying this conversation. Although my questions were entirely ordinary, I felt I was pushing her and she wasn't liking it. However, I didn't need to ask any more. I knew enough about her now to be getting on with.

"We're heading for Magdalene Bridge," I said. "We can hire a punt there. This little street we're on is called Portugal Place."

"Yes. It goes up to St. Clement's Church."

I stared.

"It does indeed. How did you know?"

"There are such things as maps," she said. "We looked at maps when we knew we were coming here."

"Oh, of course. You have a good memory, haven't you?"

"I haven't!" she said with sudden feeling. "I keep *forgetting!*" It was the first remark she'd made that sounded at all spontaneous.

"I don't think I could remember from looking at a map what street led where," I said; and then, as a kind of feeble witticism, "Are you sure you weren't prowling around last night?"

"You are very suspicious, John," she said.

"I didn't mean anything by it," I said. "Just a joke. Like when your father talked about not being bitten during the night. J-O-K-E, joke."

She didn't say anything more, but I had the sense of a slight chill between us. We arrived at Magdalene Bridge. It was still only midmorning, and there were plenty of punts for hire. Katherine got on board without hesitation, and settled herself on the cushions. I took the pole, steered the punt out into midstream, and headed upriver under the bridge.

I knew what I was doing. I am quite good at managing a punt. Actually it's only a knack, and easy enough to acquire, but people who can't do it look and feel clumsy, and people who can do it look and feel graceful, and it usually impresses visitors. It didn't seem to impress Katherine, though. I gave her the usual commentary. It's always rather brief when it comes from me, because I'm not a top-ranking authority on college histories and all that. You should hear my father when he acts as guide, which he does once in a blue moon if somebody sufficiently important comes to stay with us. When Father gets going on an architectural subject, he'll talk the tiles off a roof.

"We're passing St. John's College now," I said.

"Yes."

"That big white block on the right is the Cripps Building. It's new."

"Yes. I suppose it must be."

"And that's the Bridge of Sighs."

"Yes."

"Now we're coming up toward Trinity."

"Yes."

"That's the library. Sir Christopher Wren designed it."

"Yes."

"It's all rather good, isn't it?"

"Yes."

We passed under a weeping willow, which trailed its web of branches over the water, a trap for the unwary. Katherine moved and ducked as necessary without saying a word. Past Garret Hostel Bridge she said suddenly, "May I see if I can do it?"

"Yes, of course. Have you done it before?"

"I'm ready to try."

We stepped past each other. She stood on the platform at the back, holding the pole aloft.

"Bring it down close to the side of the punt," I said. "Keep it as vertical as you can. Then push it straight back, not out sideways. You steer by trailing the pole like a rudder."

"Yes," she said, and did it. The punt moved forward. After one or two uncertain strokes, she seemed quite at ease.

"You know something?" I said. "You're an incredibly quick learner."

No reply.

We passed under King's Bridge.

"There," I said, "under that beech tree, is where you were when I first saw you, yesterday afternoon."

And again she spoke with sudden feeling.

"Was it only yesterday? It feels like a lifetime."

It was as if she was talking of an ordeal.

six

I took the pole again as we came from under Silver Street Bridge.

"Are we going up toward Newnham Pool?" she asked.

"Yes. I live along there."

"How lovely."

"Hey," I said. "You know about Newnham Pool. You know it's a good place to live. For a stranger in this city, you know an awful lot."

"I told you," she said. "I've looked at maps and guides. We did a lot of reading before we came here."

"I bet you did. It's almost uncanny. I don't feel as if you were a stranger to Cambridge at all."

She looked uneasy at that. But I couldn't study her face, because I had to give my mind to the punt. The river up toward Newnham Pool is narrow and winding.

"This is us," I said eventually. "Our garden."

And there it was—not big, but pleasantly dappled in the June sun. Ben and Sarah sat at the silvery-gray, weathered teak table in the shade of the copper beech tree, playing a board game. Both were absorbed and serious. Neither of them noticed our approach. They must have heard the boat, but in our garden, river sounds are as common as birdsong.

We have a tiny dock, though the only boat we actually possess is an inflatable dinghy, usually tucked away in the garden shed. I tied up the punt and turned to help Katherine ashore, but she'd jumped already. Then Ben and Sarah saw us, and got up from the table. Ben, big and clumsy-looking (yet he isn't clumsy at all), went straight to Katherine. They were exactly the same height, so that he looked straight into her eyes.

And their eyes seemed to lock together. They just stood facing each other, looking, in a kind of sudden forgetfulness of what was around them. I almost had to cough.

"Ben," I said, "this is Katherine. Katherine Wyatt. And Katherine, my brother Ben. Ben Dunham."

For her that broke the spell. And almost instantly threw another.

"Ben Dunham!" she repeated. "Benjamin Dunham! It . . . it can't be!" And she was searching him with her eyes, staring at him with an interest more intense than I'd ever seen in my life.

Ben's wide brown eyes still looked straight into hers. After a moment he raised his hands and put them on her shoulders. They stayed like that for, I suppose, a few seconds, though it seemed a long, long time. Then Katherine moved back and sat down, uncertainly, on the bench beside the old teak table.

"Benjamin Dunham!" she said again. "You look quite . . ." And then she fell silent.

"Katherine," Ben said. "Hello, Katherine." Then he was sitting on the bench beside her, his eyes seeking hers again. Neither of them said anything more. I became aware of Sarah, who was standing a few feet away, watching them gravely. It was a strange, silent little tableau.

"And this is my sister Sarah," I said eventually.

Very slowly, Katherine drew her eyes away from Ben. She made me think of a swimmer coming up to the surface. "Hello, Sarah," she said, in a formal tone and with the formal smile; and then she submerged again.

I felt unaccustomedly awkward. Sarah took my hand and drew me away.

"We must leave them," she said.

"I don't see why."

"Because they are falling in love."

"Oh, come off it, kid sister," I said irritably. "We're not in a fairy story. Don't tell me it's love at first sight. There ain't no such thing."

"Yes, there is," said Sarah. She was very serious. Her eyes were wide and deep. "Katherine," she said, "has come a long way. She has come a very long way."

"I know she has. From Kingston, Jamaica, as a matter of fact."

"She has come much farther than that."

"I don't know what you mean, minnow."

"Never mind, then," said Sarah. She gave a small, very adult smile, then tugged at my hand. But Ben and Katherine were both surfacing now.

"To begin at the beginning," said Ben. "It's a fine day, isn't it?"

"Beautiful," said Katherine.

I thought of the punt, ticking time away and building up a rental bill.

"We oughtn't to stay too long," I said hesitantly. "The punt has to go back to Magdalene Bridge."

"Let me pay for it," said Ben promptly.

"No," I said. "I took out the punt. I'm paying."

"Then I mustn't keep you, must I?" said Ben. And I don't suppose he intended to. But it was an hour later, and I was feeling a kind of shamefaced jealousy of Ben, as well as alarm about the cost of the punt, by the time Katherine and I pushed off from the dock.

I knew very well what was going to happen. Laura had come into the garden, had been introduced, and within ten minutes had invited Katherine to lunch the next day. That was Sunday, and I'd arranged to go with Alan, in his ancient minivan, to spend the day with Trevor Andrews at Royston. I could have canceled that, but there wasn't any point. My absence would ease a transition that was going to take place anyway. I didn't know what Sarah meant by saying that Katherine had come a long way, but I knew she was right in her remark about Katherine and Ben. It didn't require any special insight to see that a relationship had sprung up instantly between them where I myself had failed to make any real contact.

Katherine lay quietly on the cushions while I poled all the way back to Magdalene Bridge. The thought of taking another turn seemed not to occur to her. But she looked nearer to being happy and relaxed than I had seen her before.

"Benjamin Dunham!" were the only words she spoke during the journey; and she said them in a barely audible, musing tone, to herself.

Katherine pushed open the door of the front sitting

61

room at Mrs. McGuinness's, and we went in. David and Margaret Wyatt were sitting in armchairs, apparently studying the same sheaves of paper as when I was there before.

"Hello. Did you have a good morning?" Margaret asked.

"Yes, thank you," Katherine said. And then she suddenly went tense. She was looking past David to a tiny table at his elbow. On it were a bottle of whiskey and a glass. The bottle was nearly full; obviously only one glassful had been taken from it. The glass was small, and by no means empty. It didn't look as if much whiskey had actually been consumed. But David looked as guilty as Katherine looked shocked.

"Is that . . . ?" Katherine began in an incredulous voice.

"It's whiskey," Margaret said. "David is having a drink before lunch. I shall have one too in a minute."

"Whiskey! That's alcoholic, isn't it?"

"Yes," said Margaret. "But your father and I are responsible people. A little will not do any harm."

"Certainly not," said David with an air of bravado. He raised his glass and took what appeared to be a rather small sip. Then he choked and spluttered a little.

Katherine looked as though she was about to say something more, but a glance from Margaret silenced her. There was a general air of embarrassment. Only David seemed unaware of it.

"This is very enjoyable," he said; and then, dashingly, "This evening I mean to go to a public house."

"David!"

"When in Rome, do as the Romans do," David said.

"That's an old saying. Perhaps you don't know it. We are now in Rome, so to speak, and I intend to apply it. I might even bring in some fish and chips for our supper. Fried cod and potatoes."

"It sounds unhealthy," Margaret said.

"You can't get away from unhealthy food here," said David.

"Talking of food," I said, "Laura—my stepmother—would like Katherine to have lunch with us tomorrow. I shouldn't think it will be unhealthy. Laura's pretty hot on proteins and vitamins and all that. But I shan't be there, I'm afraid. I'll be out for the day. Can I come and see you sometime next week?"

"That would be very nice, John," Margaret said. But her eyes were on David, and so were Katherine's. David took another small sip from his glass. His air was that of a small boy self-consciously enjoying a forbidden treat.

seven

Alan and Theodosia arrived promptly at nine o'clock on Sunday morning. Theodosia is Alan's minivan. She is fifteen years old, gray, and extremely battered. Alan paid thirty-five pounds for her, and I think he was robbed. She has eighty thousand miles on the clock, and I wouldn't be surprised if her true age in miles was much more than that. The arrival of Theodosia on time, or indeed at all, can't be taken for granted. Among her drawbacks is an extreme reluctance to start. Alan says she needs a rebore. I think she needs a new engine. Also a new body. In fact the needs of Theodosia are similar to those of the well-known axe that only needed a new head and a new handle.

Alan bought her the day he was seventeen and became entitled to take a car onto the public roads. By some dubious means he'd learned to drive already, and he passed his test in short order. Old and ugly as Theodosia was, Alan was devoted to her. He did need an object for devotion. There isn't much warmth in Alan's home. His father died when he was ten, and his mother married again. Two years later his mother died and his stepfather married again. So now Alan has what you might call a step-stepmother. His stepparents aren't positively unkind to him, but they're not really interested. They're both working, and they'll be glad when Alan is working, too. They could do without him, and he knows it. What Alan needs is a girlfriend, but he's a bit shy and so far he hasn't found one. He lavishes his affection on Theodosia. And Theodosia costs him much more money than a girl would.

"She'll have to have two new tires this summer," he said as we chugged along the road to Royston, twelve miles away, where Trevor Andrews lives. "The present front ones are nearly bald. I'm scared stiff of being stopped by the police. As for the spare, I'd rather not think about it."

I made sympathetic noises. Alan was silent for a while, obviously pondering this and other problems. Then he said thoughtfully, "That fellow from the Sunday paper was really interested in the people we met on the Backs."

"Oh, do you think so?" I asked casually. I had some inkling of the way his mind was working, and I didn't like it.

"I wouldn't be surprised if there was money in it," Alan said. "He didn't actually say so, but that was the impression I got."

It was the impression I'd got, too, but I didn't say anything.

"He wanted to find them, didn't he? And you weren't letting anything drop. So I kept quiet. Besides, why give him information for nothing when he might pay for it?"

"Bloody hell, Alan, they're people! You don't buy and sell *people!*"

"It wouldn't be selling people, it'd be selling information. Harmless information. If they're not doing anything wrong they've nothing to fear, have they?"

"Well, I don't think much of the idea."

"I can't see that I'm under any obligation to them," Alan went on. "In fact, quite the reverse. They gave me a fright. And the more I think about it, the more I feel there must have been some kind of drug or anesthetic involved. They *ought* to be investigated by something like Witness. You could even say it's a public duty to help this man find them."

"Oh, come off it, Alan. You want to get your hands on the money, if any, that's the long and short of it."

"I don't see any harm in combining public duty with earning a few pounds if they're offered."

I was practically gagging on all this. I reminded myself with an effort that Alan had no pocket money except what he earned from a paper route, that Theodosia was his escape from an unloving home, and that keeping Theodosia on the road was an outsize problem for him.

"Are they still at Mrs. McGuinness's?" he asked.

There was no point in lying. "So far as I know, they are," I said.

"So far as you know? You haven't seen them since the day they arrived?"

"Well . . . Yes, I was there yesterday, as a matter of fact. And Katherine's having lunch at our house today."

"Katherine? That's the girl?"

"Yes."

Alan thought all this over. Then he said, "Didn't you tell me they're an academic family?"

"Yes."

66

"So of course they *would* get on with yours. Birds of a feather and all that."

There was a bitter tone to his voice. Most of the time Alan and I get on well, being basically the same sort of people, but occasionally questions of class and background fall like shadows between us.

"Nice-looking girl," Alan went on. "I'm surprised you could tear yourself away to come to Trev's with me today."

"She isn't interested in *me*," I said.

"No? Oh well, perhaps she's a bit tall for you," Alan said nastily. I wasn't liking him much this morning.

"I quite took to the Wyatts," I said. "They may be odd, but I don't believe there's any harm in them. I wouldn't think of taking money from a Sunday paper to say where they are."

"You are holier than I," Alan said sardonically. "Also, considerably better off."

It looked as if a row was blowing up between us. Fortunately this was the moment when we arrived at Trevor Andrews's house. Signs of trouble were forgotten, and the argument was buried under a dozen other arguments, because when Trevor and Alan and I get together, what we do is argue about everything under the sun. By the time we were on the way back to Cambridge, around teatime, Alan and I had run out of talk and almost out of voice. The Wyatts were not mentioned again. I thought probably Alan was a bit ashamed of himself by now.

I was thinking plenty about the Wyatts myself, though, and particularly about Katherine. I'm not the least bit clairvoyant, but I knew what would have been happening while I was away, and I knew that however hard I tried I wasn't going to be pleased about it. It wasn't that I'd been all *that* much attracted by Katherine, and I'd realized before she and Ben set eyes on each other that I wasn't making any headway with her. It was just the old, far-too-familiar fact that Ben could always succeed where I had failed, and there were times when this was almost more than I could bear.

Alan dropped me at our gate. He could have stayed, but his stepparents, though not specially fond of his company, nevertheless considered they had a right to it, especially on weekends, and he felt he had to go home. He was just driving away in battered old Theodosia when Father arrived in his newish red Volvo. Father pipped the horn amiably at Alan, tucked the car away in a corner of the drive, and went into the house with me.

"Well," he said, "the Foster piece could have been worse. Much worse."

I realized belatedly that Terry Foster's article about the candidates for the mastership must have been in this day's paper.

"Terry doesn't have much grasp of what makes a scholar," Father said tolerantly. "Seems to think it correlates with being old, dry, and dusty, which it doesn't. But apart from that, he's got the thing surprisingly right. I'm quite glad I gave him my time, and a good dinner."

Actually the good dinner had been Laura's work, but Father wouldn't have thought of that. There was a copy of the paper on the sitting room table, open at the Witness feature. And there it all was, at the top of the page. "Away from the City jungle, Witness takes a look into a supposedly quiet academic backwater," said a line of smallish black italic type over the top of the main headline, which was THE MASTERSHIP STAKES. And four candidates were discussed. The only one to get a big picture in the paper was Father, looking very handsome, with an arm round Laura and his free hand resting lightly on Sarah's head, and lots of tree and river in the background. The other three were shown in postage-stamp-size portraits.

And the conclusion drawn by Terry Foster was that Father was the strongest candidate. He wasn't—according to the soundings Terry had taken—as distinguished a scholar as Dr. Hardisty or Professor Tillett or Mr. Seward-Anderson, but he was lively and energetic and much better known to the world at large, with far more contacts in important places.

"And fortunately he's left it at that," Father said. "He hasn't piled it on so far as to lose votes for me rather than gain them. He's just pointed out what everybody knows if they'll only admit it to themselves, namely that what matters in the choice of a master is to pick the person who will actually get things done for the college. And there isn't any doubt on that score. A pity about his remarks on scholarship, but nobody thinks a newspaperman could possibly be a judge of scholarship anyway, so it doesn't matter. I think Terry has done quite well, really."

He turned to Laura, who had just come into the room. "How do you like the thought of being the master's wife?" he asked her.

"It's not my kind of thought," Laura said dryly. "Actually I'm a teacher at a high school."

The implications of this remark weren't lost on Father, but didn't bother him.

"Quite so," he said indulgently. "You are yourself

alone. Very right and proper. My dear Laura, you are becoming a militant feminist, and I rather like it."

If I'd been Laura I think I'd have belted him one. But then I noticed that they were both looking out through the french window, which opens onto the garden. And I could see what they could see, namely Ben and Katherine swinging idly together in the garden hammock. They looked relaxed and happy and totally absorbed in each other.

Father was intrigued at once. Laura followed his eyes and said, "It's been like that all day."

"Well!" Father said. "Ben with a girl at last!"

"Yes. Strange that we've never seen him with one before."

"He must have had girl friends sometime, someplace. But never at home. A striking girl, too. Who is she?"

"Her name's Katherine Wyatt," Laura said.

"Lives in Cambridge?"

"Just visiting. I don't know for how long. But do you know, Ben's put off his return to Bristol on her account. He was going back tomorrow. Now he isn't."

"That's quite something," Father remarked.

"You can say that again. Usually he can hardly tear himself away from that lab of his long enough to come and see if we're still alive."

"Tell me more about the girl," Father said.

"I don't know a great deal about her myself. She's with her parents, and they're staying at Mrs. McGuinness's house. Her father and mother are both academics, I believe. I haven't met them. Her father is a Professor Wyatt from the University of the West Indies."

"But how extraordinary!" Father said.

"Extraordinary? Why?"

"Because," said Father, "I've been invited to visit the University of the West Indies next autumn, on my way to give that lecture at Miami."

"How nice. You didn't tell me. Will you go?"

"Oh, yes. I shan't miss a chance like that. And it will be useful to have met someone who actually teaches there. I'll be glad to hear more about the place. Why don't we call this Professor White . . ."

"Wyatt," said Laura.

". . . this Professor Wyatt, and ask him to dinner. And his wife."

"She's a professor too," I said.

"Better and better. We'll ask them both, and the girl as well. Ben will like that. Just look at them. Makes me feel quite sentimental."

"You, dear? Sentimental?"

"Don't be cynical, Laura. Even I have feelings. Actually it's quite a moment in a man's life when he first sees his son interested in a female. A stage in life's journey, to coin a phrase."

"And it's taken quite a while to reach this one," Laura said.

"I shall go out and speak to them," said Father. "I don't think it would be too gross an intrusion, do you?"

He stepped through the french window and walked across the lawn toward Ben and Katherine. They half rose and he waved them down. I watched him drop lightly to the grass and seat himself cross-legged, with hands clasped around knees, in the boyish posture he often used when talking to young people.

Katherine seemed slightly alarmed by Father's arrival.

Ben's expression was one of amiable interest, but when after a minute or so Father looked to one side so that Ben's face was briefly out of his line of vision, Ben flashed a grimace toward the french window, where Laura and I still stood. Father's pose as a youngster among youngsters had never appealed to Ben. But this was something Father was not aware of, and he wasn't suddenly going to start noticing it tonight. He would conduct the conversation to his own entire satisfaction.

As I turned away from the window, my eyes met Laura's. She'd noticed Ben's grimace, too.

"No need to worry," she said. "They won't get too much of Hugh tonight. Ben promised to take Katherine home straight after supper. It's half an hour after now, and in a minute or two I shall go out and remind them."

In fact Ben and Katherine got even less of Father's company than Laura had intended. At that moment the telephone rang. It was a call for me, from Mrs. McGuinness.

"I'd like you to come round right away," she said.

"Why?" I asked.

"You'll see when you get here. But hurry. Is Ben at home?"

"Yes."

"Get him to come, if you can. By car if possible. But not with your father. No, definitely not your father."

"Come on, Mrs. McG.," I said. "If you want me to pull all the stops out, you must tell me what for."

"It's Professor Wyatt," she said. Her voice dropped to a shocked whisper. "He's behaving *very oddly.*"

* * *

Father protested mildly at the cutting short of a pleasant evening, but when told that Ben was in default on a promise to take Katherine home he gave way with a good grace, and allowed Ben to borrow the Volvo. And within five minutes we were in Park Parade. The long June evening had not yet drawn to an end, and the cause of the trouble could be seen at once. And heard. David was sitting on the front doorstep of Mrs. McGuinness's house, singing at the top of his voice. He was drunk.

When he saw us he stopped singing, made as if to get up, then sat down heavily on the doorstep again. Margaret went to him and took his arm.

"Come on, David!" she urged him. "You *must* come inside. Do let us help you!"

"I'm not coming inside!" David said. "This is a very comfortable doorstep. I like it. I have never sat on a doorstep before. It's a totally new experience." He beamed at us.

"I have spent the evening in a pub," he announced. "A genuine old English pub. It felt like home away from home. They were nice people there. Very nice people. I drank beer and whiskey."

"Alcohol again!" Katherine said. "He's intoxicated!"

It seemed to have taken her a long time to realize what was the matter. Now she was deeply shocked. Margaret left David and came over to her.

"Try not to be too distressed," she said.

"But it's horrible!" Katherine cried.

David had burst into song again. It was about the ladies of some unknown port, who appeared to behave like port ladies in any song anywhere.

"Oh, *stop it!*" Katherine half screamed. "That *dreadful* old thing!"

"Dreadful *old* thing? It may be dreadful, but it's not old. Not now it isn't. John hasn't heard it. Have you, John? John can't have heard it. And I'm going to tell everybody why!"

"David! Quiet! I'm ordering you. Quiet!"

That was Margaret. David responded, silenced for the moment by the urgency of her voice. She appealed to us, "Please help me to get him inside."

Now David was staring at Ben.

"Who's *he?*" he demanded.

"He's Ben," said Margaret. "John's brother Ben. Let him help you into the house and upstairs."

"He's Benjamin Dunham!" said Katherine. Margaret frowned.

"Benjamin Dunham!" David got almost to his feet and gave a little bow. Then his legs folded under him and he subsided onto the step. From a sitting position he put out his hand.

"I am . . . honored," he said gravely. "A famous name indeed. You are very young, Benjamin Dunham. In fact I can hardly believe in you. Are you genuine?"

Ben was puzzled but came forward obligingly.

"You're not Benjamin Dunham really, are you?" said David. "They are—what's the phrase?—pulling my leg. They think I've drunk too much. Perhaps I have. My stomach begins to feel uncertain. I enjoyed myself, though. That was a good pub. A real old English pub. And a real old English barmaid. Very pretty. Very buxom. Though not very young."

Margaret and Ben exchanged glances, then each slid a

hand under David's arm, ready to lift him. David began singing again. "You think you'll take everything, all you fine ladies; You think you can send us all empty away . . ."

Katherine pulled a face of disgust, though the song didn't seem all that disgusting to me. I was distressed in a different way. David—tall, handsome, and supposedly a professor—had no business to be acting like a drunken oaf. There was something obscene about it.

By now Ben and Margaret were manhandling him in through the doorway. David stopped singing and suddenly became belligerent.

"I will not be treated like this!" he proclaimed with drunken dignity. "Even if you are Benjamin Dunham— which I doubt very much—you have no right to push me around. As for *you*, Margaret, it is all very well for Sonia to put you in charge, but please remember we are now in a male-dominated society, and I am a dominant male!"

"We're going upstairs," said Ben gently.

"Don't tell me where we're going," David said, "or I shall . . . I do believe I shall *hit* you."

"David!" Katherine almost shrieked.

And David himself now seemed to feel he had gone too far. Or perhaps the uneasiness of his stomach was increasing. In spite of his brave words, he allowed himself to be half pushed, half pulled up the stairs by Ben and Margaret. Katherine followed them into the house, and the door closed behind them. Mrs. McGuinness and I were left outside.

"Well!" said Mrs. McGuinness. "How do you like that?"

"I'm sorry, Mrs. McG.," I said. "I didn't think

anything like this would happen."

"I'm sure you didn't, John. But it *has* happened, hasn't it?" She went on thoughtfully, "I do know a certain amount about gentlemen. Remember, I was a college bedmaker for fifteen years before I started working for your family. And there's no denying it, gentlemen do have a drop too much to drink from time to time. I've put gentlemen to bed more than once before now, and been thanked for it the following morning. But a real gentleman is always a gentleman, even if he *has* had a drop too much."

"What are you getting at, Mrs. McG.? Do you mean to say that Professor Wyatt doesn't behave like a gentleman?"

"Oh, I wouldn't go as far as that. I'm sure he's a real gentleman where he comes from. But I don't think he's used to our ways. Carrying on like that; and him a professor, too! No, I wouldn't say he's not a gentleman, but I do say it's not the way any of *our* gentlemen would behave."

"Well, as I say, I'm sorry. I meant it for the best when I brought them here."

"It's not that *I* mind so much, John. But the neighbors . . . And I don't know what Mr. McGuinness will say. He must have heard all this carrying on. I'm surprised it didn't bring him out, and him with his leg, too. I can't have this sort of thing going on, John, I really can't."

"What can I do?" I asked her.

"I'd be glad if you'd tell them, any more behavior like that and they'll have to go, they will really. I'd rather you told them than me. And I'd hate to have to give notice to friends of yours, but I might have to. You understand, don't you, John?"

"I understand perfectly," I said.

The door of the house reopened, and Ben appeared. He said a rueful "Hello" to Mrs. McGuinness, and an almost immediate "Good-bye" as she disappeared toward the rear quarters of the house. He looked harassed, and mopped his forehead with a tissue.

I tried to make a joke of it all.

"Are you the real Benjamin Dunham?" I asked him. "Or are you an impostor?"

"I couldn't understand those remarks he made," Ben said. "What's so special about being Benjamin Dunham?"

"You'd better ask Katherine," I said. "You seem quite special to her."

I'd meant to say that lightly, but it came out with a hint of bitterness. I don't think Ben noticed, though.

"Poor Katherine," was all he said.

"I don't think David's been like that before," I said. "She seemed quite shattered. Not at all as if she was used to it. Her mother took it a bit better, but it seemed to shake her, too."

"Poor souls," said Ben.

eight

Monday, the day after the scene with David Wyatt, was the first day of examinations for me, and for Alan as well. There's something to be said for exam time at our school, because they only make you go in when you actually have an exam. If you have one in the morning only, you get the afternoon off; or the other way round. Or you may get the day off completely. But as it happened, the first day of these exams was a brute, with sessions both morning and afternoon. So my nose was well and truly applied to the grindstone, and I didn't have time to think about the Wyatts. They hadn't been mentioned at breakfast. At suppertime both Father and Laura were at home but Ben wasn't.

Halfway through the evening, Father said casually, "I suppose he's out with that girl."

"Yes," said Laura.

"Oh, well, it had to happen sooner or later. I hope it doesn't distract him too much from his research. By the way, have you invited the Whites to a meal?"

"Wyatts," said Laura. "No. Sorry, dear, I forgot.

Actually I think it might be nicer to send them a note, rather than telephone them at Mrs. McGuinness's, especially as we haven't met them. I'll write one now. Ben or John can take it in the morning."

Father and Laura had both gone to bed by the time Ben came in. They thought I should have been in bed too, but I thought otherwise. It was a little after midnight when Ben arrived, and he looked irritated.

"Fancy having a man like that for a father!" he said. "He's a menace."

"David?"

"Yes. Of course. David. Professor bloody Wyatt. I can't understand him at all. I wouldn't have thought it possible for a grown man to behave the way he does."

"What's he been doing now?"

"Well, when I got to Park Parade this morning the learned professor had quite a hangover, and serve him right. To do him justice, he did at least seem ashamed. He was full of excuses for what had happened and assurances that it couldn't happen again. We left him on the sitting room sofa, nursing his head and feeling repentant. And then, believe it or not, when we got back this evening there was a note to say he'd gone to the pub!"

"Don't say he was drunk again!"

"No. It was odder than that. I went round at once to see what was happening. And there he was at the bar, as large as life. He was only drinking tomato juice, but he was making quite an exhibition of himself, buying drinks for everyone in sight, and flirting with the barmaid. Then he got into a darts game, but he hadn't a clue on how to throw straight. He was barely hitting the board. I kept well out of the line of fire, I can tell you."

"At least I don't suppose you had to bring him home."

"Not exactly. He could walk perfectly well. I don't think he'd touched a drop. But it was just as well I was there. He wanted to see the barmaid home and was making himself a bit of a nuisance. I persuaded him to abandon the idea. I don't think he actually had designs on her, he was just pretending to be a devil of a fellow."

"It's a funny business, isn't it, Ben?"

"It's weird. I just don't know what to make of David Wyatt. He acts as if he's playing some kind of game. At large in Merrie England—except that this isn't Merrie England. He's having fun in a way, but it's as if it wasn't real to him. As if it was a stage set, perhaps."

"Anyway, have *you* had fun?" I asked.

"Oh yes, apart from that. A quiet day, really. We just did some sightseeing, in the city and out on the Roman Road. Margaret was with us part of the time."

"What? Her mother came too?" I raised an eyebrow. Ben was slightly embarrassed.

"Well, Margaret's interested in architecture and antiquities and all that. . . . I had to watch them in the traffic, though. I've never come across people with so little sense of self-preservation. They were scared stiff of everything on wheels, and even so they blundered and nearly got themselves run over."

"There's something odd about all three of them, isn't there, Ben?"

"There's something very odd," said Ben. "And yet . . ."

"And yet you fancy Katherine."

"That's not how I'd put it," said Ben. He was silent for

a while, his expression remote, almost dreamy. I suppose when they fall late they fall heavily.

"What exams do you have tomorrow, John?" he asked eventually.

"None at all. A day off."

"Well, listen, I'm hoping to borrow the car and drive Katherine to Ely. I think we're entitled to a day on our own. But I'm a bit worried about Margaret. Things are rough for her. And then there's David. He wants watching. John, could you bear to come to Park Parade in the morning and rally round?"

"Oh, great!" I said. "You go out with the girl, and I look after her mom and dad!"

"Never mind," said Ben. "Forget it. Sorry I spoke."

"It's all right," I told him. "You picked your victim well. Self-sacrifice is my besetting sin. We'll play it your way. But take my advice, Ben Dunham. Never get yourself an older brother. They're a pain in the arse."

Ben didn't even take a pretended swipe at me.

"Thank you for your help," he said. "I do appreciate it."

I gave him a look that ought to have sent him straight through the floor, but he didn't even notice.

Actually I was quite willing to go and see Margaret again. I still rather liked her. I wasn't so sure about David. But it was on my mind that I ought to give them that warning from Mrs. McGuinness. And when Tuesday morning came, everything worked out smoothly. Ben dropped Father at the college, drove on to Park Parade, collected Katherine from the doorstep, and left me at the

Wyatts' with Laura's invitation clutched in my hot little hand.

I tapped at their door and went in. Margaret came straight across to greet me. She put her hands on my shoulders.

"It's good to see you, John," she said. "You and Ben have been so helpful to us. And I'm afraid we've given both of you a difficult time."

"If you mean the other night," I said, "it doesn't matter at all. Honestly it doesn't. At least, it doesn't matter to Ben or me."

"You mean it does matter to somebody?"

"Well . . ." I began. I was embarrassed, but this gave me an opportunity to get it over and done with. "Actually, yes. Mrs. McGuinness says if there are any more scenes like that you'll . . . you'll have to go."

Margaret sighed.

"I'm not surprised," she said. "I can't blame her. I wish it hadn't happened. We're in a complicated situation, and that kind of thing doesn't help. I only wish I could tell you what's actually going on—but you wouldn't believe me if I did."

At this point David came in from the bedroom. His step was brisk and his manner cheerful.

"Hello, John, how are you?" he said; and then, to Margaret, "Did I hear the name of McGuinness just now?"

"Mrs. McGuinness says," Margaret told him in a steady, deliberate voice, "that if there are any more scenes we shall have to leave."

"How typical of the woman," said David lightly. "Well, she needn't worry. There won't be any repetition.

Just an isolated occurrence. Such lapses have been known to happen, even in the best of circles. Surely we don't need to talk about it."

I was willing enough to move on to another subject. I said to both of them, "I have a note for you, from my parents."

I handed Margaret the envelope. She took out the note and studied it for some little time.

"Can't you read the handwriting?" David asked.

"I do find it rather difficult," Margaret said.

This was a little odd. Laura is generally reckoned to have a very clear hand. But after a few seconds Margaret said hesitantly, "It's an invitation to dinner. From Hugh and Laura Dunham." She paused, frowning slightly, then added, "Mrs. Dunham says it has been a pleasure to meet Katherine, and that her husband would particularly like to talk to us because he is going to the University of the West Indies this autumn."

"Is he indeed!" David said. He and Margaret looked at each other. I detected an almost imperceptible shaking of heads.

"It would be nice to meet some people," Margaret said. There was a trace of wistfulness in her tone. David turned to me.

"Please thank your parents for their invitation," he said. "We shall be replying to it."

I suspected that the Wyatts meant to turn it down. I didn't know why.

David had sounded less amiable than before, and I didn't understand that, either.

"We are building up quite a connection with your family," he said thoughtfully. "You found us this place to live. Then there's Ben's friendship with Katherine. And now a dinner invitation from your parents, which would imply even closer acquaintance." He spoke as if these were dubious benefits. "And your father is going to the West Indies. That's very interesting indeed."

There was a pause. Then David appeared to change the subject completely.

"You know," he said to Margaret, "I think I ought to have my treatment."

"Your treatment?" said Margaret; then, "Oh, yes, perhaps you should. Today, do you think?"

"This morning," said David. "In fact, why not now?"

Margaret turned to me.

"David has to have treatment for his back," she said. "He has a little trouble with it, John, as you may have noticed."

Actually I hadn't noticed any such thing. But I tried to sound sympathetic.

"Is it serious?" I asked.

"It's not all that serious," David said.

"But he does need the treatment," said Margaret. "It's rather tiresome and painful for him, I'm afraid. I have to give it him. And it takes a little time."

I can take a hint. "I think I'd better go," I said.

"I don't *want* you to go," said Margaret. "Not at all. But just for a while . . . yes, perhaps it would be better."

"All right. Good-bye."

I felt sour. Everybody wanted me out of the way today. First Ben, now Margaret and David. And I had an odd feeling that, whatever troubles David might have, there was nothing wrong with his back. The suspicion was ridiculous, of course. Why should they pretend a thing like that? Was it really very odd that a bad back didn't happen to have been mentioned before on the few occasions when I'd been with them? Of course it wasn't. Yet the strangers seemed to be surrounded by small mysteries. I was beginning to find it trying.

Margaret must have read something in my face.

"Don't go away for good," she said. "Come back in an hour's time and stay to lunch. And John, dare I ask you a favor? There's a book on old Cambridge that Ben recommended. I have the author and title written down here. Would it be any trouble to you to go and buy me a copy?"

I brightened.

"No trouble at all," I said. "And I can pass that hour by browsing in the bookshop."

"Or by having a cup of coffee," Margaret said. "Take it out of the change." She gave me a crisp new five-pound note.

I felt more cheerful as I left the house in Park Parade. Perhaps I wasn't totally unwanted after all. The sky, which had been gray, was lightening, and there were just-perceptible shadows. Jesus Green lay in front of me, its trees still fresh with early summer brilliance. The tennis courts were in use, and the light thud of tennis balls and the calling of scores came floating across the green. Beyond was the river . . .

Then, from the corner of my eye, I noticed two figures disappearing round the side of the row of houses and out of my view. One of them at least was familiar, very familiar. The other looked slightly familiar, too.

I wasn't in any hurry this morning. Something moved

me to walk a few yards along the street, away from the now-vanished figures, and to sit down on the low wall of a garden, more than half hidden by somebody's lilac tree. I waited there for a minute or two. Then one of the figures reappeared. And yes, it was just who I thought it was. Alan Stubbings.

nine

"Alan!" I called. "Alan!"

Alan was embarrassed, and looked for a moment as if he might turn tail. But he waited for me to come up to him.

"What are you doing here?" I demanded.

"I could ask you the same," he said, without much conviction.

"Well, there's no secret about what *I'm* doing," I said. "I've been visiting the Wyatts. The people we met on the Backs the day of your great disappearing act. They're living at Mrs. McGuinness's, as I seem to remember telling you. I'm going out to buy a book for Mrs. Wyatt, and then I'm going back there for lunch. That's *me* accounted for. Now tell me what *you're* up to."

"Oh, just walking around," he said uneasily.

"And it's sheer accident that you're practically on the Wyatts' doorstep?"

"No, I wouldn't say that. I was quite hoping to catch sight of them. I was interested, but I can't claim to be a friend of theirs, like you."

"O-ho. And who are you with?"

"What do you mean, who am I with?"

"You know what I mean. There was somebody with you a minute or two ago."

Alan didn't say anything to that.

"I'm going to tell you who it was," I went on. I took a deep breath. I thought I knew, but I wasn't quite sure. "It was Terry Foster, from the Witness page."

The way Alan went red, I knew I'd scored a hit.

"All right," he said. "It was Terry. So what?"

"I'd like to know what you're both doing here, that's all."

"It's not your business, John."

"Yes, it is. Terry told both of us he'd like to find the Wyatts. I wouldn't give him any information. Obviously *you* have. You thought there was money in it, didn't you? Well, was there?"

Alan was still red-faced, but his tone was defiant.

"Yes," he said. "There was. A little."

"I hope you can stand the smell of it," I said.

"Don't use that high moral tone with me, John Dunham. I'm not under any obligation to the Wyatts. And it's all very well for you to talk. Your family's not short of money. I can use all I can get."

I knew that was true. I bit back the remark I'd been on the point of making. Instead I said, "Where's Terry Foster now?"

Alan didn't say anything, but indicated a pale blue Audi standing at the curb a few yards along the street. The man at the wheel was partly concealed by the newspaper he was reading. But as we approached the car he stepped out and sauntered toward us.

"Hello," he said easily.

"Hello, Mr. Foster."

"Terry."

I felt hostile toward him.

"I gather you got your information," I said. "By paying for it."

"Correct," said Terry. "Newspapers do pay for information occasionally. Information is our stock in trade, after all. Do you object?"

"I think you're prying into people's lives," I said.

"Not so. I'm not concerned with people's private lives. I'm only concerned with what they're doing if it affects the public interest."

"And what have the Wyatts to do with the public interest? They're just visitors to Cambridge. Ordinary visitors, like thousands of others."

"Not altogether ordinary," said Terry. "From what I'm told, it seems they're of striking appearance and they arrived almost literally out of the blue."

"So? It doesn't sound like much of a newspaper story to me. Unless you're going to tell me they come from Alpha Centauri."

Terry smiled.

"I'm not in the science fiction business," he said. "All right, I'll tell you why I find them interesting. You see, we have two rather curious reports lying on our news desk. They're from journalists in two other towns, both of which, by coincidence—or perhaps it's not coincidence— have ancient universities. One's from Oxford. It seems that a research student, name of Shirley Unwin, was sitting reading in Exeter College garden the other week. She felt a little odd—slightly dizzy, as a matter of fact."

Terry looked hard at both of us as he said this, then went on.

"She looked up and noticed two elderly ladies a few yards away, who also seemed to have been suddenly affected by something. Then Shirley Unwin lost consciousness—very briefly, she thinks; only for a few seconds. And when she came round, the two old ladies had vanished. But there in the garden were—"

"Tall mysterious strangers," finished Alan.

"Yes. Three of them. They hurried away hastily in the direction of the street, and up to this morning nothing more had been heard of them. Shirley Unwin was baffled, but she was more shaken than baffled. And she'd just about convinced herself that nothing unusual had happened except that she'd had some kind of mental aberration, when the dizziness came over her again. And next minute the two old ladies were back on the college lawn. They seemed to be all in a dither, and not to know what was going on."

"Seems to me," said Alan, "that I know just how they felt."

"Shirley Unwin went over and spoke to them," Terry said. "They were totally incoherent, and she couldn't get anything out of them that made sense except their names. They were a Miss Jessica and a Miss Lucilla Makepeace, daughters of a Professor Makepeace who died many years ago, and they were still living in their father's house in North Oxford."

"How did your news desk hear about this?" I asked.

"News desks do tend to hear about things. Shirley

90

Unwin was so struck by this incident that she went to the police, but she couldn't get them interested. That's understandable, since nobody was hurt or missing and no damage had been done. I don't suppose they saw any need to go and listen to the maunderings of a pair of old ladies. They seemed to think Shirley herself was a nut case, for which you can't blame them. In fact she was beginning to think so herself by now. But her boyfriend happened to have a friend who was a freelance journalist, and he was more interested than the police were. Also, he was in touch with us . . . It's a curious parallel, isn't it? An extraordinary parallel."

Neither of us said anything.

Terry went on, "I've been to Oxford and talked to Shirley and the old ladies. There's not a lot to add. The old dears were extremely confused, and they seemed to think they'd been away a long time, and possibly out of Oxford. They kept saying 'It was so different,' and then 'It was so much the same.' I gave it up in the end. But the three strangers haven't been seen. At least, they haven't been seen in Oxford."

"So that's why you're interested in the Wyatts."

"Of course. The Durham story is more extraordinary still. The police up there found there were forged five-pound notes in circulation. Extremely accurate forgeries, superbly printed on good crackly paper and numbered in series. A brilliantly professional job. It was a bank cashier who noticed it; and pretty sharp of him, too. A difference of texture, mostly, I think. Only an observant person handling notes all the time could possibly have detected it, but once suspicion was aroused there were other tiny

91

differences that could be spotted. And the Bank of England soon confirmed it. No such series of notes had ever been issued."

"And the connection?" I asked, though I was beginning to guess it by now.

"Well, this time there were no reports of mysterious disappearances, nothing like that. But the banks were looking out for forged notes as they came in, and every one was traced back as far as possible. In most cases that wasn't far. But three or four notes were found to have been used for payment in shops and stores that had some recollection. And those that did have a recollection had rather similar recollections."

"Tall dark strangers?"

"Yes. Three tall, dark strangers. They had been passing themselves off as academics, but inquiries showed they were nothing of the sort."

"And were they found?"

"No. The police were very close to finding them. Once they thought they'd tracked them to a house near the cathedral. They couldn't get any reply, and went for a search warrant. And when they *did* get in, the place was empty. That was early last week. Since when, no progress."

"Are you suggesting," I asked, "that the Wyatts are connected with these other two incidents?"

"Well, it does seem possible, doesn't it?"

"Then surely it's a matter for the police," said Alan.

"If there *is* any connection, then yes, of course it is. But I don't want to set the police on harmless people. That's why I'd like to see them myself before I do anything else."

"I think," I said slowly, "that *you* think there's a really big story behind this. I don't think a simple banknote forgery, or mysterious strangers in college gardens, would interest Witness, unless you thought you were onto something much more important. Huge-scale international fraud, or spying, or political cloak-and-dagger work—isn't that more in Witness's line?"

"I've told you a lot," Terry said. "I'm not telling you anything more. But what I *am* going to do is call on your friends. Now, this minute, if they're at home."

"Oh, they're in all right," I said. "David's having his back rubbed, or something like that." And the sheer harmlessness of such an activity increased my feeling that Terry Foster must be making a ludicrous mistake.

"I don't think there's anything the least bit sinister about the Wyatts," I went on. "They couldn't be involved in fraud or forgery or whatnot, they simply aren't the type. And as for being tall and dark and so on, well, Professor and Mrs. Wyatt both teach at the University of the West Indies. I just don't know what people in the West Indies look like."

"They teach at the University of the West Indies?" Terry said. "You're sure of that?"

"Well, that's what they told us."

"I can easily check it," said Terry.

This was the moment at which it dawned on me, belatedly, that if there was a connection with the Durham incident, and if the people there had only been pretending to be academics when they weren't really any such thing, then the odds were that the Wyatts were also phonies.

Or even the same phonies?

And the still more unnerving thought struck me that the

93

Wyatts, too, were putting five-pound notes into circulation. I had one of them in my pocket at this moment. Supposing these, too . . .

Involuntarily, my hand flew to the pocket I'd put the note in, and I felt it between my fingers. Could it be a forgery? My heart gave a little bump.

I looked across at Terry, and saw that he was studying my face. He couldn't of course have guessed about the five-pound note . . . could he? I wondered if my cheeks were as white as they felt.

"Wait here a minute," Terry said quietly. He got back in his car and it slid away.

Alan and I looked at each other. I took the offensive.

"I think this stinks," I said. "Police, Sunday papers . . . ugh!"

"Listen, John," said Alan. "If the Wyatts are on the level, they'll soon be able to prove it. If they're not on the level, Terry'll expose them, and a good thing, too. That's a public service. I'll be glad I was able to help."

"And collect the money," I said.

"Oh, get stuffed."

"You know something, Alan Stubbings? In another minute I'm going to knock your block off."

"Are you, Shorty? You and who else?"

We were quarreling like small boys, and for a moment it seemed that we might fight. Then I suppose it struck both of us at once that we were getting too old for that kind of thing. We glowered at each other for a minute or two before Terry returned, surprisingly soon.

"I've only been as far as the nearest phone booth," he said. "I spent two minutes and two coins there. It was time and money well spent, too. One call was to the public library here. They're very helpful and efficient. And I'll tell you what they told me. As of last summer, there was nobody called Wyatt on the teaching staff of the University of the West Indies."

"They could have joined more recently," I said.

"Quite true. They could have. We shall see. I also called my office. I knew they had a full report on the Durham affair, and I thought it might be interesting to have the numbers of the forged notes that were found there." He handed me a scrap of paper with some figures jotted on it. "If any of the Wyatts happen to give you a five-pound note, John," he said, "compare its number with these."

"Why should the Wyatts start giving me five-pound notes?" I asked.

This was a bit of bluff, and I regretted it almost at once, because it put an idea into Alan's head.

"You're buying a book for them, aren't you?" he said. "Did they give you money for that?"

"What if they did?"

"Not a fiver, by any chance?"

"I'm not here to answer questions," I said.

"That's all right," said Terry. "I'm not going to interrogate you. But if you do get a note, compare it, and if there's too much resemblance, please tell me. I know you feel friendly toward these people, but loyalty has its limits, and abetting a forgery is beyond them."

He looked at me with an odd, diffident half-smile.

"It's a funny old world we live in," he said, "and it has some funny people in it. If you had my job for long, you'd know how often things aren't what they seem on the surface. I really do want to meet your Professor Wyatt,

John. Take me in and introduce me, there's a good chap."

"I don't see why I should," I said.

"I shall see him sooner or later," said Terry. "Wouldn't you rather be there when it happens? Then you'll know just what questions I'm asking him. I think that's what you'd prefer."

"All right," I said. "That's if David Wyatt will see you."

"If I were a friend of his," said Terry, "I think I'd suggest that it might be better for him if he did."

ten

"John!" said Margaret Wyatt. "You've only been away twenty minutes."

"I know. You said an hour."

"And these people." She looked in some surprise at Alan. "Isn't he the boy who . . . ?"

"Yes, he is," I said. "His name's Alan Stubbings."

"He's still all right, I hope?"

"I'm perfectly all right," said Alan.

"And this," I said, "is Terry Foster, from the Sunday paper. The Witness page."

"A journalist," Margaret said. She sat down, slowly, on a hard chair. "From an important newspaper?"

"Very," I said.

"What do you want?" she asked Terry. Her tone was level but reluctant.

"I just wanted to meet you," Terry Foster said. He gave her the diffident half-smile. "And Professor Wyatt."

"David's having his treatment, isn't he?" I asked.

Margaret said nothing.

"For his back," I went on. "Actually I thought you were giving it to him."

"He's gone out," Margaret said.

I stared.

"But . . . how *can* he have? I've had your door in sight ever since I went out of the house."

"You must have missed seeing him," Margaret said. There was weariness as well as reluctance in her voice.

"What about his back?" I asked.

"He decided to have the treatment later."

I didn't believe Margaret. But I still liked her. I thought she wasn't much of a liar, and I had a strong sense that her present shiftiness went against the grain of her personality.

"A pity," said Terry pleasantly. "I was hoping to meet him. I understood he was Professor Wyatt of the University of the West Indies."

Margaret said nothing.

"Perhaps I can see him some other time," Terry suggested. "When will he be back?"

"I—really don't know."

"He *will* be back today, I suppose?"

"I'm sorry, I have no idea."

"Oh, well," Terry said. "I shall just have to keep trying, shan't I? There's no great hurry. I'm staying in Cambridge for the present. At the University Arms. If the professor would care to call me there when he comes in, I'd be very much obliged."

"What is it about, Mr.—er—Foster?"

"Oh, it's just that I'd like to have a general discussion with him about what he's doing."

"He's on vacation here, that's all," Margaret said, with more energy in her voice than before. "He isn't doing anything in particular, except a little sightseeing."

"I'd like to meet him, all the same," Terry said. "I shall be in Cambridge until I do." He gave his engaging smile. "Do tell him so. But for the moment I won't trouble you anymore."

Terry's voice was mild, without the slightest trace of threat in it. But I had the sense that there was steel underneath. He meant just what he said, and he meant Margaret Wyatt to know it. He would stay around until David had talked to him.

I didn't leave the house in Park Parade with Terry and Alan. There was something I had to check, and if necessary to think about, before I said another word to them. As soon as they'd disappeared down the stairs I excused myself and went to the bathroom. I took out the five-pound note. Then, with a flutter of butterflies in my stomach, I groped for the scrap of paper Terry had given me.

Of the two letters and eight digits in the serial number of Margaret's note, only the last two digits differed from those of the forged banknotes found at Durham.

I can't say this surprised me. I'd been more than half expecting it. Even so, it shook me more than I'd have thought possible. I tried for a moment to tell myself that the similarity might be accidental. But that was ridiculous. It was far too close for coincidence. Under the circumstances there couldn't be the shadow of a doubt. The note Margaret had asked me to change was a dud.

I swallowed hard, clenched and unclenched my fists half a dozen times, and went back into the Wyatts' sitting room. Margaret was standing in the big bay window. I went across to her. She looked into my eyes, slightly downward, with her dark, deep, intelligent ones.

"Where *is* David, actually?" I asked.

Margaret moved away from me without speaking and sat down on the sofa. I looked out of the window onto Jesus Green. The sun had momentarily left it as a cloud shadow passed across the grass, but you could see sunlight again beyond the shadow. A tennis player threw the ball up, hit it into the net, threw a second ball up and served again, then darted across the court to take the return. Through the side pane of the window I saw Terry and Alan talking together, twenty or thirty yards along the street toward Terry's car. I wondered what they were planning to do now. Though I felt that Terry Foster and I were on different sides, I didn't dislike him. He was just a newspaperman doing his job. There was something formidable about him, all the same.

Margaret hadn't answered my question. I repeated it.

"I told you, John, David isn't here. He went . . . away."

"It still seems odd that I didn't see him."

"You don't believe me, do you? And neither did your newspaper friend. I'm sure he thought that David was hiding somewhere—in the bedroom or bathroom perhaps. But he was quite wrong. David really is not here at the moment." She sighed. "I don't know why anyone should think he would hide. For that matter, I can't understand why our movements are of such interest."

"I'm afraid they *are*," I said. "And I don't find it surprising."

I put my hand in my pocket and drew out the five-pound note.

"Do you really want me to spend this?" I asked her.

"What do you mean, John?"

"Listen. I'd better be blunt about it. I think this note is a forgery."

"John!" Her face was white now. "What makes you think that?"

"Never mind why I think it. Is it true?"

No reply.

"It is, isn't it?"

She stared at me and said nothing. I was still watching Terry and Alan. Now they separated, and Terry went back to his car. Alan remained leaning against the railings on the Jesus Green side of the street. A moment ago I'd been feeling that Terry and I were on different sides. Now I wondered whether this was really true.

"It's not very nice, being asked by somebody you thought was a friend to pass a forged note," I said.

"I'm not admitting anything, John. I can't."

"Seems to me you don't need to admit this," I said. "It speaks for itself."

"Oh, John . . . I can't go on like this. I don't know what to say to you."

"You're involved in a racket, aren't you?" I asked brutally.

"Not a *racket*, John."

"What, then? If passing forged notes isn't part of a racket, what is it?"

"I wish I could tell you. Oh, how I wish I could tell you."

"Well, I expect the world will know before long," I said. "The Witness team doesn't fool around. Terry Foster thinks he's onto a story, and so do I. And I think he's the sort of person who won't give up till he's got it. Every bit of it."

"John," she said. "We're not involved in anything dishonest. At least, it's supposed not to be dishonest. There's an explanation. But I can't—truly I can't—give it you."

"I don't see how anyone can explain forged notes away."

"The money isn't genuine, I know. I don't really understand about that. They told us nobody would know and no one would ever lose by it."

"*They?* Who's *they?*"

"John, I absolutely cannot tell you."

"There's too much you can't tell me," I said. "And listen, whatever anyone says, of *course* passing forged notes is dishonest. You've paid for rent and food and drink with dud money, haven't you? That money's in circulation. Somebody's got to lose by it in the end."

"Not if it's never discovered."

"But it's *been* discovered. At least, money like it has been discovered. And the police are onto it! In Durham . . ."

"*Durham!*"

"You know something about Durham, then?"

"Yes, it's similar." She stopped short.

"Similar to what?"

"I mean it's an old university town, that's all. Similar to Cambridge and Oxford."

"Something funny's been going on in Oxford, too. Do you know anything about that?"

"Oh, don't *drive* me, John. What with this and David, I'm so tired . . . We shall have to go. I know we shall have to go."

"Go where?"

"Go from here."

"Where to?"

"London, perhaps. Though we might have to go altogether."

"What do you mean, altogether? Back to the West Indies?"

"Perhaps."

"Where you and David teach?"

"Yes."

"But you don't! There are no Wyatts on the staff of West Indies University!"

There was a hunted look in her eyes now.

"London's a big place," she said. "People disappear in London."

"Maybe. But not so easily with Witness after them. I think you'll find Terry Foster takes a lot of disappearing from. To say nothing of the police. And then there's Katherine. You know how things are. What will happen to Ben and Katherine?"

"Oh, what a mess!" she said. "That's the worst part of all. Much worse than the money. That's tragic!"

Then she was crying. Suddenly it struck me that there was a look of my mother about her, though I don't know why. I've only seen my mother in photographs. I suppose if my mother had been alive they'd have been about the

103

same age. Against my own intention I went over to Margaret and put my arms round her.

"Tell me!" I said.

"I can't!" She was shaken now with sobbing. "I can't, I absolutely cannot!"

"Can David?"

"No."

"Where is he now? Really?"

"He's gone. That's true, at least. He is not here. Not at this moment."

I stood holding her, totally baffled. Then I realized that the five-pound note was still in my hand.

"Here," I said. "Take it. I don't want anything to do with it. I haven't seen it. I don't know it exists. I don't *want* to know it exists. And don't ever give me money again."

She took the note and tore it in tiny pieces. And as I watched her do so, I began to feel traces of the dizziness that had come over me on the Backs. Margaret seemed to feel something, too.

"It's time you went," she said.

"What's going on? What in heaven's name is it all about?"

"You have to go!" she said. "John, you must go!"

I stared at her.

"You understand plain English, John? Go!"

My knees were weak. I stumbled somehow to the door. Margaret was actually shoving me from behind. The door slammed, leaving me half-collapsed on the landing outside. Through the whirl of my dizziness I heard David's voice, then hers, raised in what sounded like an altercation.

104

"What was all that?" he was demanding crossly.

"That was John. He nearly got caught up. Never again in this small space, David. It isn't safe."

So he *had* been in the house all along, hiding from everybody!

I'd have been inclined to beat on the door and shout "I heard you!" if I hadn't been so weak with dizziness. I tried to pull myself together but couldn't stand straight. I heard David's voice again, but the words were undistinguishable. Then came Margaret's clear tones, "All right, David. You must go on and do it. And quickly. Tomorrow. This *is* an emergency. We can't use the money we brought with us anymore!"

I staggered dangerously down the stairs. As I moved away from the Wyatts' door the dizziness began to lift. And as it did so I felt more and more furious. Forgery was a criminal matter. It wasn't for me to protect the strangers against the consequences of that. Worst of all I felt, illogically—they weren't playing straight with me, weren't coming clean. Not even Margaret. To hell with them.

I made my way into the street and half collapsed onto the low wall outside. Alan came running up to me. He was concerned.

"Do you feel any of that dizziness?" I asked him.

"No." His tone was one of surprise. "Do you?" And I realized that I didn't; it had lifted already.

"Not now," I said. "I did a moment ago . . . Alan, what are you doing, still hanging around here?"

Alan was shamefaced.

"If you want to know, John," he said, "I've decided you were right after all. I shouldn't have done what I did. It's just that Theodosia costs such a lot to keep on the road. I was tempted and fell. I've told Terry I regret it. I tried to give him his money back, but he wouldn't take it."

I was startled. My own feelings were moving in the opposite direction. For a moment I couldn't say anything.

"Don't rub it in!" Alan appealed to me.

"If you want to know," I said, "I was just thinking that Terry's right and the Wyatts are crooks, and perhaps I ought to have been helping him!"

Suddenly we were both laughing, without much amusement.

"Seems to me," Alan said, "that we've both been wrong in opposite ways. And the best thing we can do now is to leave Terry Foster and the Wyatts to their own devices. Shake!"

He put out his hand. I shook it.

"I'm going home now," Alan said. "I still have some studying to do for tomorrow's exam. I'm going to forget about all this."

"I wish I could," I said. "I can leave Terry Foster to his own devices, that's an easy trick. But the Wyatts are another matter. I suppose you know that Ben's besotted with Katherine? What am I going to do about that?"

eleven

I didn't sleep well that night. Partly it was because of worry about Ben. He came in very late—late enough for Father to make apprehensive remarks about the fate of the Volvo, to say nothing of the fate of his elder son. I didn't get a chance to talk to him before going to bed. And if I had, I wouldn't have known what to say. I couldn't bring myself to tell him, "Ben, the girl you're going out with comes from a family of crooks." And I didn't think he'd believe me if I did.

In the next day's mail there was a letter which Father read at the breakfast table with apparent surprise.

"Extraordinary!" he said. "They're not coming!"

"Who aren't?" Laura asked.

"The Wyatts."

"Why not?"

"Professor Wyatt's in poor health, according to his wife. She doesn't say what's wrong with him, though, or how long it's likely to last. And she doesn't say anything about hoping to meet us some other time, or any of the usual sweeteners. In fact it's a bit brusque. You could almost call it a snub.''

"Well, well," said Laura.

"Well, well, indeed," said Father. "Perhaps I'm being immodest, but my name is not unknown. Most people visiting Cambridge would jump at an invitation to dine with us.''

"Maybe we're not as famous in the West Indies as in England or America," Laura suggested. There was a dry note in her voice.

"I don't think that's so," Father said, rather sharply. I realized that he was quite offended by the declining of his invitation.

"Actually," said Ben, "Professor Wyatt *has* been a little under the weather in the last few days.''

I shot a suspicious glance at Ben, wondering what exactly he meant by "under the weather," but his eyes were innocent.

"Thank you, Ben," said Father. "You have of course a familiarity with that establishment which is denied to me.'' This time Father's tone of voice was distinctly sour. I decided that by now he was sufficiently curious about the Wyatts to feel frustrated as well as snubbed. And another thought occurred to me. Though Father was a well-known figure, a television pundit, and a leading contender for the mastership of his college, he had never been made a full professor at Cambridge. There were some on his faculty who were said to be doubtful about his standard scholarship, though Father's own belief was that they were merely jealous. He was inclined to be resentful of people less well known than himself who had the title that had been denied him.

"I think Professor Wyatt's just very tired," Ben said diplomatically. "I believe he's been overworking for a long time. And Mrs. Wyatt is worried about him. Perhaps that's why her note seemed curt."

Father grunted and let the subject drop. He had to go to London that day to make a broadcast, speak at a luncheon, and give an afternoon lecture. He'd be back in Cambridge in the early evening. By his standards it wasn't a specially hard day; he might have had to go to a dinner or give an evening speech as well. It was surprising that a person as busy as Father could spare as much thought for the Wyatts as he did. Ben drove him to Cambridge station and came back half an hour later with Katherine in the Volvo.

Katherine was thoughtful, a little withdrawn from the rest of us. I wondered if anything had been said to her about yesterday's developments. If so, she gave no hint of it. But there was an air of quiet understanding between her and Ben that rather impressed me. What lay between them was nothing you could put your finger on, exactly; just a sense of unspoken harmony, and, when their eyes met, an opening out to each other, an almost imperceptible moving together. It felt as if they were lovers. Whether or not they were lovers physically I couldn't tell, but in some deep quiet way they were in tune with each other.

However, after a long day together yesterday, they didn't seem this morning to be seeking each other's exclusive company. They had, it seemed, plenty of leisure to talk to Laura, and to Sarah. Laura doesn't have to teach on Wednesdays; and as Sarah isn't strong, and is apt to be exhausted by a whole week at the bustling local elementary school, she's sometimes kept at home on Wednesdays too. This particular morning, Ben said, "Katherine and I are going upriver in the inflatable. Sarah, would you like to come with us?"

Sarah's eyes lit up. Any other child of nine would probably just have said "Ooh, yes!" and that would have been that; but Sarah, though clearly delighted, was thoughtful. After a moment she said in her precise, rather grown-up little voice, "Yes, I'd like to, if you are quite sure you don't mind."

"Of course we don't mind," Ben said. "We want you, minnow. That's why we asked."

Katherine hadn't said anything, but she was still thoughtful, and she now looked at Sarah with a curious tenderness. "Please come," she said, and gave Sarah the rare, nice smile that had so appealed to me when I first saw it.

There was a great hustle, getting the inflatable dinghy out, wiping dust off it and finding an air pump to blow it up; and then they were away. I wasn't among those invited, which was reasonable, because the inflatable isn't meant to hold more than two adults. Sarah was so small and light she hardly made any difference. And anyway, I had an exam the next day, and it was more than time for me to do some preparation.

It was a fine day, sunny though not warm, with a light breeze. I could have worked at the teak table in the garden, under the copper beech tree, but that calls for too much self-discipline; there's always something happening on the river to distract your attention. So I retreated to my own bedroom, where I slogged away doggedly for the rest of the morning.

Toward one o'clock I became aware that there was someone else in the room. I looked round sharply, to see Sarah sitting on my bed.

"Hello," I said.

"Hello, John."

"What can I do for you?"

"Nothing, John. I only came to say that lunch will be ready in five minutes. I've been watching you work."

"That must have been a thrill."

"And I came to tell you something. I have just had the happiest morning of my life."

"Congratulations, minnow. How did you manage that?"

"It wasn't anything *I* did, John. It was just being in the dinghy with Ben and Katherine. Everything was so beautiful, and they were so happy."

"Have you been fairy-storying again?" I asked. "Imagining princes and princesses and all that?"

"Oh, no, John." Her eyes were wide. "This was real, ever so real. We just paddled up the river, in the shade, under the great green trees. Past Robinson Crusoe Island and Paradise and Swan Island and Dead Man's Corner."

"Well, those sound like names out of stories."

"But they're not. You know they're not, they're just places on the river. And then through Grantchester Meadows. And Ben told Katherine the names of all the flowers."

"Yes. Ben's good at wildflowers."

"And I picked some for Katherine. Only common ones, of course, that wouldn't be missed. She thought it was wonderful. Anyone would think she'd never seen

111

wildflowers before. And we saw a kingfisher."

"Go on! Did you really? I've never seen a kingfisher on this river in my life."

"We did. It was a special, special day. I knew that, even before we saw the kingfisher. I shall never have such a happy day again."

There were tears in her eyes.

"Don't be silly, minnow, of course you will. Come here."

I hugged her. She's a slight, frail-looking child, not like most of the kids who bounce around our district bursting with health. "You'll have lots of happy days," I told her, "lots and lots. That's for sure. Now let's go and see what we're having for lunch."

We were just sitting down at the table when the telephone rang. It was David Wyatt, and he wanted to speak to me.

"John?" His voice was cheerful. "How are you? Yes, I'm fine. Yes, so is Margaret. John, I think you've been getting some wrong ideas. I'm horrified at what you must be thinking of us. Come to supper this evening, and let me explain."

"Have you seen Terry Foster?" I asked.

"I've *seen* him. I haven't spoken to him. Actually I'd rather speak to you first. I'd have said 'Come at once,' but I'm just leaving for Newmarket. I'm going to the races."

"You're *what?*"

"I said, I'm going to the races. You wouldn't have me come to this fair city and not go to Newmarket Races, would you?"

It sounded to me like fiddling while Rome burned.

"Listen," I said. "I think you're in all kinds of trouble. Surely Margaret told you. Terry Foster and the Witness page are only the beginning."

"I know what you have in mind, John. But that's all nonsense. I'll tell you about it later. Or . . . if you're not at school today, why don't you come to the races with me?"

A possible explanation flashed into my mind.

"You're not by any chance thinking of betting on horses with nice new five-pound notes, are you?" I said. "Because if so, you can count *me* out, for one."

"You're imagining all that crime-novel stuff about five-pound notes," David said.

"I wasn't imagining when I saw a whole wad of them in your wallet," I told him.

"John, at this moment I have not a single five-pound note in my possession. Nor has Margaret. Anyway, we can't discuss this foolish topic on the phone. Come to the races with me if you can. If not, I'd like to see you this evening."

"Ben's here now," I said. "And Katherine."

"Oh." A pause. Then, still lightly and cheerfully, "Bring them along, too."

I was about to make a sharp retort when it struck me that David at the races was potentially an even more disastrous phenomenon than David at the local pub. If he really was going, it would do no harm for Ben and me to go with him. I didn't care all that much what happened to David himself, but in spite of all the indignation I'd felt yesterday, I did still rather care about Margaret and Katherine. And so far as I knew, Ben and Katherine didn't have any other plans for this afternoon.

113

"I'll ask them if they'd like to come," I said.

In the end, all four of us went to the races—David, Ben, Katherine, and I—in Father's Volvo. What Father would have thought of this I didn't know. Ben said he'd be amused when he heard about it. I wasn't so sure. But it was Ben who was in charge of the Volvo, so I wasn't going to worry too much about that.

I'd never been to a racetrack before, and didn't really know what to expect. I had in my mind's eye a vague recollection of that well-known *Derby Day* painting, an impression of fairground bustle and surging colorful crowds, and a jumble of memories from the television screen of horses racing neck and neck. And in my mind's ear, so to speak, was a sound track of a racing commentator galloping to a crescendo of excited gabble. I wasn't expecting what I did find—a wide open, windy place with a cluster of modern buildings, paved areas, and escalators, rather like an airport.

David was in high spirits. You'd have thought he hadn't a care in the world. He paid with well-used one-pound notes for us all to go into Tattersall's enclosure.

"No nice new fives, you notice," he observed cheerfully to me. I could hardly ask where he'd got the money from, but I supposed it must have come to him in change. And obviously he didn't have much more. When he'd bought a race card he smoothed out a last, very crumpled pound note.

"This," he said, "is now my worldly wealth. I must try to increase it by successful betting."

By now I was past being surprised at anything David said. I decided I might as well put the various mysteries out of my mind and just enjoy the racing.

Inside the enclosure the scene was more as I'd imagined. There were bookmakers standing on what looked like soapboxes, chalking figures on boards or shouting the odds in incomprehensible terms, and there were tic-tac men frantically wagging their hands to convey mysterious messages to other parts of the track. Most of the actual betting seemed to be going through an official institution called the Tote; people lined up at windows, handed over money, and were given little tickets. I didn't think this would appeal to David, with his taste for colorful England; and it didn't. "I shall place my bets with bookmakers," he declared, "or bookies, as I believe they're called."

I noticed that he had a daily paper folded open at the racing page, and had made marks of some kind against the names of horses that were running in various races. It seemed he'd been studying the form. Extraordinary, I thought, for a professor of history, but there was no accounting for tastes. I did however see several notices on bookmakers' boards saying the smallest bet they'd accept was one pound. If David lost his pound note on the first race, that surely would be the end of the proceedings for him.

Katherine had shown no interest in bookmakers or betting, but when a little knot of horses galloped past the enclosure, moving quite rapidly on their way from the parade ring to the start, she looked up with immediate interest.

"So those are the horses!" she said.

"Yes, dear," said David; and then, "You have seen horses before."

"Of course," said Katherine, and, after a pause, "Aren't they beautiful?"

"Undoubtedly," David said.

Katherine didn't look at all anxious. By now I'd come to the conclusion that whatever David and Margaret might have told her about yesterday's events, they hadn't told her they were in trouble.

Ben wasn't showing much interest in anything but Katherine.

The first race was about to start. David studied the board near the finish line which showed the names of the runners.

"Aspidistra," he said, "is the favorite, at five to four on. That means—doesn't it, John?—that if I put my pound on Aspidistra I shall win a mere eighty pence?"

"Yes," I said. "That is, if Aspidistra wins. But Aspidistra might not win, and then you'd lose your pound. Why don't you put your money on something else? Look there's a horse at twenty to one. If you put your pound on that and it won, you'd get twenty."

But David wasn't interested in the horse at twenty to one.

"I shan't bet on this race," he said.

The start was a long way from the stand from which we were watching. A voice over a loudspeaker said the horses were in the stalls, ready to go, but all you could see was a row of dots. And when the commentator shouted "They're off!" you could still only see a row of dots. Then the row of dots became a bunch of dots, then a bunch of larger dots, and the larger dots grew and resolved themselves into tiny animals, and the tiny animals grew and grew and their hooves began to be heard as they drummed toward us. And then they were streaming past us in line, each horse and rider as one, raked forward into the wind, flowing, almost flying over the track, their element the air around them rather than the ground beneath. And in seconds it was over.

"How lovely!" Katherine said. "How completely lovely!"

"And Aspidistra comes in first by at least half a dozen lengths," said the voice over the loudspeaker.

"Well, you'd have won your bet," I told David.

"Not worth it," he said casually.

Everyone seemed to be drifting from the stand to the paddock, where stableboys and girls were already leading the horses entered for the next race round the parade ring. Katherine, towing Ben by the hand, almost ran to see them. To me it seemed there was a sorry contrast between the beauty of the horses and the lack of beauty of the racegoers. Indeed the horses, meticulously groomed, with their air of lofty breeding and their long, spindly legs, looked a little awkward and out of their true medium when merely walking.

David studied the card again. There were a dozen runners for the second race, and it seemed more to his liking.

"I shall stake my pound on John of Gaunt," he declared.

"There's a horse in this race called Port Royal," I pointed out. "Isn't there a Port Royal in Jamaica?"

"What?" said David; and then, after a brief pause, "Yes, indeed. A stronghold of pirates in the seventeenth century."

"Why don't you have a flutter on Port Royal, then?" I suggested. "It might bring you luck."

But David stood firmly by John of Gaunt.

The horses were now being ridden by their jockeys round the parade ring. I thought David might like at least to look at John of Gaunt and Port Royal, but he didn't show any inclination to do so. We moved back into the stand, leaving Ben and Katherine still watching the horses.

"We must find a bookmaker," David said.

There were about twenty to choose from, and they came in all shapes and sizes. One at least was lean, austere, and scholarly in manner; another looked like a small, prim accountant. David, as I'd expected, went to the man who looked most like the stout, red-faced, cigar-smoking bookie of traditional cartoons. After listening carefully to the two or three customers in front of him, he announced that he was putting a pound on John of Gaunt to win. The odds were six to one against. When the race began, five minutes later, they had lengthened to seven to one. Apparently John of Gaunt wasn't getting much support. David was unperturbed.

This was a longer race, and the start was far away, out of sight to anyone without binoculars. By the time the horses came into view, one of them was far ahead of the field. It was John of Gaunt, and it stayed in front all the way. Ben and Katherine watched with eager interest. My heart pounded as hard as hoofbeats. But David wasn't paying much attention; he appeared to find the crowd more interesting than the race. John of Gaunt won easily. David collected his winnings with quiet satisfaction. Ben was impressed and Katherine mildly surprised. Port Royal finished nearly last.

The third race was won by an odds-on favorite, but again David showed no interest. He waited until the fourth race, then put the six pounds he'd won on a horse called Unburnt Boats, at seven to two. Unburnt Boats won handsomely and increased David's capital by twenty-one pounds. Ben was now full of astonishment and admiration.

"How do you do it?" he inquired. "Do you really know about racing? I suppose you must."

"I read a little about today's races in the paper," David said; and then, "If you have a pound to spare, Ben, put it on Fields of Amaranth for the next race. That's at ten to one. The best odds of the day." Ben listened respectfully to this advice, and put his pound on Fields of Amaranth without hesitation.

In fact Fields of Amaranth was well behind the leaders for most of the race. I thought David had come unstuck at last. Then right at the finish Fields of Amaranth came up strongly on the outside, and was one of four or five horses that surged past us, so close together they looked like a blurred photograph of the same horse. I couldn't have told who'd won, but the commentator declared at once that Fields of Amaranth had got his nose in front, and so he had. David collected two hundred and fifty pounds from his chosen bookmaker, who gave him a searching look but paid up manfully and even patted him on the back. Ben pocketed a tenner with much satisfaction.

David had a double whiskey in the bar before the last race.

"Observe the caution with which I now approach this stuff," he said. "I do rather like it, all the same." Then he went on, "I'm putting my two hundred and fifty pounds on Paracetamol. And I shall spread it around among the bookies."

"David," said Ben, "isn't that risking rather a lot? You

could put, say, fifty pounds on Paracetamol, and still go home with a handsome profit, even if he loses."

"Paracetamol," said David, who was now in high good humor, "will not lose, I assure you." And his two hundred and fifty pounds, split among five different bookmakers, all went on Paracetamol to win. By the time of the start, the odds of two to one against Paracetamol were down to six to four. It was a short race, only five furlongs, and was over almost before it began. David was hardly even watching. The horses were closely bunched, and once again I couldn't see who had won. But by now I had such faith in David that I was staggered when the loudspeaker announced that Moby Dan had finished first. Paracetamol was second.

I was not so shaken as David, though. He simply couldn't believe it. He rummaged in his pocket for the racing page from the daily paper, and examined the pencil marks he'd made. Then he said, "Yes, I was right. It should have been Paracetamol."

His face was white.

"But this is ridiculous," he said. "This is incredible."

"You've lost all your winnings, haven't you?" I said. "What rotten luck, David." And although I didn't hold any brief for David Wyatt, I couldn't help feeling sorry for him.

Then there was an announcement on the loudspeaker. An objection had been lodged against Moby Dan. David relaxed and beamed again.

"Of course!" he said. "It had to be that!"

He didn't seem greatly on tenterhooks during the next few minutes. And he wasn't surprised at all when the objection was sustained and Paracetamol was declared to be the winner. He picked up his winnings, about four hundred pounds.

"I think we can consider this a successful afternoon, don't you?" he said, as we all got into Father's Volvo.

There was no denying that. David now had far more money than he could get into his wallet. His pockets literally bulged with notes. They were ordinary notes, many of them creased or soiled. None of them, it occurred to me, could give rise to the slightest suspicion of forgery.

twelve,

On the way back from Newmarket to Cambridge, David's spirits rose even higher. He sang, in his pleasant tenor, two or three songs I knew and two or three I didn't, including the one about the port ladies, from whom it was apparently necessary to escape in a ship of some kind I hadn't heard of.

Katherine grew more and more embarrassed. At last she appealed to him. *"Please,* David, stop it. You make me ashamed!"

"You're unduly puritanical, my dear," David said. "This is not a puritanical age." And he broke into a song that sounded salacious even to me. But as the car entered Cambridge he said, "However, I daresay you and Ben can manage without my company for the evening. Ben, why don't you take Katherine out to dinner? I'll give you ten pounds. I suppose you can still get a meal for ten pounds?"

"Actually I *have* ten pounds," said Ben, "from the bet I won." And he wouldn't take any money. But he volunteered to drive David and me to Park Parade before going off with Katherine for a meal.

"Don't forget you have to pick Father up at the station," I reminded him as I got out of the car.

"Not so," said Ben. "Father told me this morning he had an appointment with that Witness man, who's staying at the University Arms. And the Witness man—what's his name? Foster?—is meeting him at the station. So I don't have to bother."

I made a face as Ben and Katherine drove away. I didn't like the sound of a meeting between Father and Terry Foster. That had the ring of trouble to come.

Meanwhile, here I was at Park Parade because David had said he wanted to talk to me; but David wasn't thinking of that at the moment. He didn't appear to be in a mood to talk seriously to anybody about anything. He marched into the house, made his way upstairs, and threw open the door of the Wyatts' front room. Margaret was sitting at the table, apparently studying one of the sheaves of printed papers that I'd seen before. She looked drawn and worried.

David crossed the room, beaming, and kissed her.

"Oh, *David!*" she said. "You promised me . . ."

"I assure you," said David, "that I've only had one drink all day."

So far as I knew that was quite true. David was extremely high on his own success. He thrust his hands into his pockets and pulled out bundles of banknotes, fastened with rubber bands.

"Just look at that," he was saying, "and that, and that!"

Margaret looked but didn't say anything. In a minute or

two the end of the table was covered with money.

"Winnings!" said David. "That's what they call it, winnings! Forget about the other banknotes. They were rubbish. This is real." He picked two or three bundles up and stroked them lovingly. "There are plenty more," he declared, "where those came from. If I need some more, I shall—" he struck an attitude of extreme self-confidence—"I shall go and *win* some more." He burst out singing again. "You think you'll take everything, all you fine ladies . . ."

I realized that Margaret was on the point of weeping. I thought I'd better try to cheer her up.

"David's been lucky today, hasn't he?" I said.

"Lucky?" said David. "*Lucky?*" He was indignant. "You don't collect money on this scale by chance. I knew what I was doing, I assure you!"

"David! Stop that, please! And remember, John is our guest. John, I hope you have a good appetite. Supper will be ready in a few minutes."

Then the doorbell rang. I heard the slapping of Mrs. McGuinness's slippers on linoleum as she shuffled to the front door to answer it. There were footsteps on the stairs, and voices. Familiar voices. A tap at the door. David began hastily gathering money together and shoving it into the sideboard. Only the sheaf of papers that Margaret had been studying remained on the table.

"Come in!" David called, after an interval that seemed a long one but could only have been a few seconds. And in came my father and Terry Foster.

Father, as was his habit, moved straight in to take the center of the stage. Terry, quiet and unobtrusive, slipped round to the back of the table that occupied the middle of

124

the room. Something there had caught his eye. I realized that it was the sheaf of printed papers. He put out a hand and drew them gently toward him.

"Professor and Mrs. Wyatt, I presume," my father said. His confident, rather loud voice seemed to fill the small room. There was a perceptible stress on the word "Professor."

"That's correct," David said. Father strode to him—it was only a couple of strides—and thrust out his hand. The gesture was oddly aggressive, as if his intention were to strike. David extended his own hand, and Father shook it emphatically.

"My wife is also Professor Wyatt," David said. Father turned to Margaret with a brief "How-do-you-do." Then he indicated Terry, who was standing at the far side of the table, reading. In contrast to Father, Terry looked small and insignificant.

"This gentleman," Father announced, "is Mr. Terry Foster, of the Witness team. You know about Witness, of course, Professor Wyatt?"

"I have heard of it," David said. No doubt Margaret had told him of Terry's previous visit. But in any case Father wasn't one to miss an opportunity for making an impressive statement.

"Witness," he said, "is the prime example of investigatory journalism in this country."

"And why," asked David, "have I the honor of a visit from Witness?"

That was a question for Terry, but Father didn't wait for him to answer it. "Witness finds you very interesting, Professor Wyatt," he said, "and so do I." The last four words were spoken with some emphasis, and Father added, in the tones of one reaching the climax of a pronouncement, "I, by the way, am Hugh Dunham."

David sat down. He'd sobered up rapidly. I could see that he was alarmed.

Father looked as though he were acting the part of a courtroom lawyer. "I suppose, Professor Wyatt," he said, "that you are new to your post?"

David said nothing but raised his eyebrows in a question.

"I suppose this," Father said, "because your name does not appear on the list of staff of West Indies University in the Commonwealth Universities Yearbook."

"In the nature of things," David said mildly, "such books cannot be entirely up to date."

"Quite so," said Father; then, "By coincidence, I'm expecting to give a lecture there next autumn. Your head of department, as it happens, is an old colleague of mine. His name is—oh, dear, remind me of his name, will you, Professor Wyatt? It's gone right out of my head."

He stared challengingly at David. I could tell at once that this was a test, and that David was going to fail it. He didn't know, or had forgotten, the answer.

Margaret took over.

"I'm sorry, Mr.—er—Dunham," she said, "but I don't feel my husband should be expected to submit to this interrogation. He is not very well this evening."

This gave David a momentary breathing space. He recovered strongly. "That is so," he said. "I really cannot talk to anyone just now. Could you perhaps come back some other time instead? And preferably give me notice of your visit?"

"No," said Father, with a hint of pugnacity. "We could

126

not come back some other time instead. There are matters we should like to discuss with you *now.*"

"I am afraid," said David coldly, "that this is quite impossible. I am sorry, but I must ask you to leave my premises."

"Then you must ask in vain," Father said. "Because, as it happens, these are not your premises, they are *my* premises. Mrs. McGuinness is my tenant."

"Then perhaps," said David, still fighting, "you will not mind if *I* leave *your* premises. I feel the need to take a walk. I may be out for some time. Margaret, I should like it very much if you were to come with me."

"Before you go," said Terry, very quietly, "I rather wish you would let me have your comments on what this sheet of paper says. It might be in your own best interest to do so."

"That?" said David. He recognized the sheaf of papers. "Those papers are confidential. You've no business to read them!"

Terry took no notice. He was holding the papers firmly in both hands. He read aloud from the top sheet in his soft, barely audible voice.

"You are from the University of the West Indies, where you have been on the teaching staff for the past year. The university has its main campus at Mona, on the outskirts of Kingston, Jamaica. It has at this time an academic staff of approximately seven hundred, and about seven thousand students, of whom more than half are at the Mona campus. There are colleges in Trinidad and Barbados which also form part of the university. The subject you teach is your own. You must familiarize yourself with the state of development of your subject at the relevant time. Notes on the social and physical characteristics of Jamaica are attached, and should be committed to memory.

"It is thought that you are highly unlikely to encounter anyone who is actually teaching at the university. Should you do so, it is most probable that he or she will be a member of a different faculty, in which case your statement that you have been there for only a year will be sufficient reason for nonacquaintance. The possibility of your meeting someone from the same faculty is so remote as to be virtually nonexistent. Should that happen, you would have to say there was some misunderstanding, and remove yourself rapidly on whatever pretext came to hand.

"You have already been fully briefed on your age, background, and family circumstances. Do not forget that . . ."

Terry made to turn to the next sheet, but David was leaning over the table toward him, white-faced.

"Give me those papers!" he demanded. "They are mine!"

Without a word, Terry pushed the sheaf of papers across to David.

"Why did you do that, Terry?" my father asked, disappointed. "Just when it was getting so fascinating."

"They *are* his papers," Terry said mildly. "Besides"— with a slight smile—"I had taken a glance ahead. There's only some more of the same. Quite interesting, but not really adding anything to our knowledge."

"Who are these instructions *from?*" Father demanded, in a loud voice.

128

"I have no comment to make on that," David said. His voice was steady.

"The notes are anonymous," said Terry, "as might be expected."

There was a brief silence. Then David said, "Come along, Margaret. We will go now."

"I shouldn't, if I were you," Terry Foster said.

Ignoring him, David stood up once more and pushed his chair back.

"Sit down, please," said Terry. His voice was still soft, but there was a steely note to it. David glanced across at Margaret, who hadn't moved. Then, slowly, he sat down.

"Thank you," Terry said. "That was wise of you. You have a great deal to explain, and I think you would be well advised to explain it to me."

"Say what you have to say, Mr. Foster," said David. "And I will explain what I see fit to explain."

"Thank you," Terry said again, dryly "Now, to begin with, Professor Wyatt, or whatever your name really is, you are a phony. An impostor."

"I am not an impostor," David said with some dignity. "My name is David Wyatt, and I am a professor."

Terry was not disconcerted. He smiled and said, "Very well. I'll accept that you *are* Professor Wyatt."

"Thank you," David said with a touch of sarcasm.

"That, however, is not the respect in which you are a phony," Terry went on.

"David!" said Margaret. "We shall have to go. Completely. You know we shall."

"You'll have to 'remove yourselves rapidly on whatever pretext comes to hand'?" Terry Foster quoted. He smiled. His manner was quite friendly. "Please don't," he said. "And not just because it's less tiresome to talk to me than to the police. We're approaching an extremely interesting point."

"Then let's get to it!" said Father, who was growing impatient.

"Very well," Terry said. "Professor Wyatt, you and the two ladies arrived in Cambridge last week . . ."

"You mean my wife and daughter," David said. "Their names are Margaret and Katherine Wyatt, as everyone has been told. Is it the usual practice of your newspaper to take so little on trust?"

"I apologize," Terry said smoothly. "Professor Wyatt, you and your wife and daughter were first seen on the Backs at King's College by two high school boys, John Dunham here and his friend Alan Stubbings. You seemed, they said, to appear from nowhere. When Alan Stubbings spoke to you, he had an extraordinary experience in which he himself seemed to disappear, and afterward was under the impression that he had been in Cambridge by night, although it was broad day. At about the same time, a parallel report reached our office of a similar occurrence in Oxford, in which it was said that three people suddenly appeared and two elderly ladies temporarily disappeared."

David had turned away as if uninterested, but I knew that in fact he was listening intently.

"You and your wife and daughter," Terry went on, "are all three unusually tall and, if I may say so, strikingly handsome."

"Thank you for the compliment," David said. "It is

not, so far as I know, an offense under English law to be tall, or even to be handsome."

"Indeed it is not. It's a characteristic which, according to our reports, you share with the people who appeared in a college garden at Oxford. However, let's stick to Cambridge for the moment. The three of you were first seen on the Backs with your hand baggage, not yet having found a place to stay. That itself is a curious minor fact. Most visitors to a city surely find their hotel or whatever it may be first, and get rid of their baggage before they go out sightseeing."

"Once again," said David, "there is not to my knowledge any law which prohibits anyone from doing as we did."

"Correct. There's no law against it. It's merely a little surprising. Similarly, it's only a little surprising that you were alarmed by the street traffic, and that you were unfamiliar with the methods of hiring and paying for a taxicab."

"This is really rather boring," David said.

"Perhaps. And it must have been an awful bore when Katherine put your clothes in the drier at the laundromat and they melted."

I was surprised.

"It's the first I've heard about *that*," I said.

"It happened, did it not, Professor Wyatt?" Terry asked.

"What if it did?" said David. "One never knows what clothes are made of these days."

"Not quite so," Terry said. "They're supposed to say on the label what they're made of. And although there are a good many synthetic fibers in use, I don't know of any that would melt in the heat of a clothes drier."

"Hey, Terry, how did you find out about that?" I asked.

"A bit of guesswork," Terry said. He smiled. "There was a paragraph in the *Cambridge Evening News* the other day about a laundromat owner who found a gooey mess in the bottom of one of her driers. She said it came from clothes brought in by a tall girl who, when she came back and saw what had happened, looked very embarrassed and hurried away. Fortunately the lady seemed to think it rather funny. But when I read about it I thought of the Wyatts and wondered if there could be a connection. It seemed worth a shot in the dark. And it appears I scored a hit. Did you complain to the makers of the clothing, Professor Wyatt?"

"Life's too short to worry about such matters," said David.

"No doubt. But now we come to a more serious affair. My newspaper heard from Durham that three people pretending to be academics had been passing five-pound notes, and mysteriously disappeared when the police began to look for them."

"I can assure you that *that* has nothing to do with us," said David.

"I wonder," said Terry. "I've been worrying a little about this. Supposing forged five-pound notes had been put into circulation in Cambridge during the past few days? Should I not be obliged to do something about it?"

"And have you any reason to suppose that forged notes have been circulating here? Or, if they have, that they have anything to do with us?"

"I have no actual evidence," said Terry thoughtfully, "but I have deep suspicions. I think it possible that John may have some information."

I didn't say anything but, infuriatingly, I could feel my cheeks going red.

"What did you do with the five-pound note you were given to make a purchase, John?" inquired Terry.

"I've never admitted I was given one," I said.

"However, I think you were."

"I gave it back," I said.

"A pity. That was equivalent to destroying evidence. I wish you had kept it."

"The fact is," said David, "you have nothing to go on whatever. All you are talking about is vague and wild suspicion." He had bounced back completely now, and was looking confident again. "Anyone who wishes may search me and my premises. They will find no forged banknotes here. I have quite a large number of banknotes around, but they certainly are not forged. I am not in need of money."

"He won lots of it at Newmarket Races," I said.

"Oh!" Terry looked thoughtful. Then, "You backed several winners?" he asked.

"Yes, I was fortunate."

"Extraordinary!" Terry said. "I shouldn't have thought that racetracks were your natural habitat." He pondered for a moment. Then his face cleared. "But of course!" he said. "How obvious! Yes, of course, of course! Splendid!"

Father had been uncharacteristically quiet for a few minutes. "It may be obvious to *you*," he said now, "but I must admit I'm still baffled."

"I have just become much *less* baffled," Terry said. "How many winners did you back, Professor Wyatt?"

"It's none of your business," said David, "but there isn't any secret about it. Four."

"And no losers?"

"No."

"A remarkable degree of success."

"It's not all *that* unusual, is it?" I asked.

"Extremely unusual, I think," said Terry. "Not so much in itself as in the way it was achieved. Professor Wyatt, I believe the secret of your success was simply that you knew in advance which horses were going to win."

"O-ho!" said Father. "So *that's* what he's up to. Which is it, Wyatt—ringers, doped horses, or some other kind of racetrack fraud?"

David just stared at Terry without saying a word.

"I don't think there's any kind of fraud in that sense," Terry said. "I think the truth is much stranger. I think—" his voice was barely audible now, but everyone was listening intently—"I think the reason you seemed to appear from nowhere is because, so far as we are concerned, you *did* appear from nowhere. I think the reason for Alan Stubbings's experience on the Backs is that he got caught, so to speak, in the slipstream of some process that I don't pretend to understand. I think that the reason why you were alarmed by traffic and unacquainted with taxicabs is that you come from an environment in which they are unknown. I think your clothes melted in the drier because they were imitations, made from fibers that somebody had not realized would react adversely. I think that forged five-pound notes were supplied to you by somebody, as they were also supplied to the people in

Durham who have not been found. I daresay before long we shall hear of forged five-pound notes in Oxford."

Terry paused for a moment. Nobody said anything.

"The racetrack winnings are the oddest but the most enlightening phenomenon of all. I think, Professor Wyatt, that you knew which horses would win because you were in a position to go and look up the results before the races started. I am beginning to think I can make a shrewd guess about where you come from. I was on the wrong track in doubting your identity. I believe that you are indeed Professor David Wyatt. I am inclined to guess that the university at which you are a professor is Cambridge."

"Ridiculous!" my father burst out. "He certainly is not!"

"Perhaps I should have said," Terry went on gently, "the university at which David Wyatt *will be* a professor is Cambridge. In the year two thousand two hundred or thereabouts."

"David!" Margaret groaned. Her expression was desperate. But David himself smiled, with something like relief.

"As a matter of fact," he said, "it is two thousand one hundred and forty-nine. You are half a century out, Mr. Terry Foster. Nevertheless, I congratulate you on a remarkable piece of deduction. A unique piece of deduction, in fact. Substantially, your facts are correct. May I ask now what you propose to do with the information? Publish it in your paper? How many people do you think will believe a word of it?"

"Not a soul," said Terry. "Least of all my editor."

thirteen

David was still smiling, as if by bringing things into the open Terry had eased him of a burden. He seemed quite relaxed. In contrast, Margaret was tautly wound up. You could feel the tension in the air around her.

But the most startled person present was my father. David's admission had taken him aback even more than Terry's exposure. He looked from one to the other, unable to believe either of them.

"Am I in a madhouse?" he asked.

"We are all quite sane, I assure you," said Terry.

"Then it's some kind of hoax. It doesn't strike me as very funny. Will someone please tell me what this business is *really* about?"

"Mr. Dunham," said Terry, "I believe every word of what I have just said."

"It's extraordinary," said Father, "what an intelligent person can bring himself to believe." He went on, with an air of enormous patience, "Listen, I'm not a mathematician or a philosopher, but I know enough about it to understand that the notion of time travel is absurd. It might be possible to *repeat* the past if, as many people say, it's all still there somewhere. Conceivably you could play it over again, like running through a tape. But you couldn't insert yourself into it, as these people claim to have done."

"I don't claim anything," David said. "I'm not here to claim things. Mr. Foster made an allegation and I've admitted it, that's all. You don't have to accept my admission. You can believe I'm some kind of racetrack crook if you prefer."

"Frankly," said Father, "that's just what I do believe."

I wasn't as skeptical as Father was. I suppose that some such explanation as Terry's had been hovering round the borders of my mind for quite a while and I'd been reluctant to let it in; it was too wild. But now that Terry had put it into words, it carried conviction. It made sense of so many puzzling incidents. All the same, there were problems.

"I see Father's point, David," I said. "Or at least, I think I do. If you really come from Cambridge in 2149, this is the past for you, and the past is *fixed*. It's in all the books and records. How can you possibly move people back and let them start tampering with it?"

"That's two questions," said David. "How you can move people through time is largely a technical problem, and it's been solved; I know it's been solved for the best possible reason, namely that it's been done. It's been done to others as well as to us. Incidentally, it isn't done with any kind of machine or gadget, it's done by a form of highly intensified concentration in which the people who are moved have to take part. Only a minority of people have the capacity to do it, and even fewer actually get the chance. But basically it's simple. The question of tampering with the past is much more difficult."

"Yes, it is, isn't it?" said Terry. "Because everything that's being done is continually affecting everything that's *going* to be done. Take Mrs. McGuinness, for instance. She now has lodgers, namely you, that she wouldn't otherwise have had. As a result, the rest of her life won't be quite the same as it would have been if you hadn't come. Or take an even better example. Ben Dunham is out with Katherine this evening, and I understand he's become fond of her. Now if a young man falls in love, it surely alters his life, whether anything comes of the affair or not."

"Don't worry about that," David said. "It's not too difficult, really. When we leave this time, we shall restore. Or rather, the powers-that-be will restore. I don't understand the detailed workings, but at least the principle's straightforward. The people in charge of the experiment will put things back as they were. Just as if nothing had happened."

The word "experiment" made me sit up.

"You're taking part in an experiment?" I said. "What is it? What are you doing? Finding out about *us?*"

"Oh, no. Historians of my day know all they want to know about you. More than they want to know, perhaps. Yours, to be frank, is not one of the great ages of humanity—not by any means."

"Then if you aren't interested in us, what are you doing?"

"I wouldn't say *I'm* not interested in you. Personally I find life in your time quite fascinating. But the twentieth century has been fully explored and is very well documented. In fact, for us, your century is not much more than a training ground."

Margaret had looked increasingly uneasy as David went on speaking.

"David!" she said now. "You know we're not supposed to talk about what we're doing."

"My dear," said David, "we have failed in our task already. We've been detected, and that's that. When we report back to Sonia, we shall be recalled. Am I right?"

"Yes," said Margaret. "No doubt about it, I'm afraid."

"So we can't do any harm now. As far as we're concerned, the experiment's over and we shan't get any more chances. And anything we tell people now will be forgotten when restoration takes place. We have nothing to lose."

"Sonia won't like it."

"Sonia's not going to be pleased with us anyway. I can't see that this will make much difference."

"Do tell us," Terry said.

David took a deep breath.

"As you've gathered," he said, "we're historians. Social historians. Our concern is with the way people used to live. And time-shifting is the best research tool ever developed for social history. Think how much can be learned by actually going into the past that could never be got from documents. Researchers who can mix undetected with people going about their daily business can find out what life was really like."

"You said something about a training ground."

"Yes. That's what the twentieth century is. The times we're really interested in are the ones farther back, which we know so much less about. But the farther back they go,

139

the more the researchers need practical experience. The ways of life—and thought and speech—are so much more distant from ours. You have to be an expert to pass muster. Especially in view of the height problem. You'll have noticed that we're taller than most of you; well, we're *much* taller than people of a few centuries before you. That makes it hard to be inconspicuous. And there's yet another practical difficulty. The farther back you go, the more likely you are to suffer from time lag."

"Time lag?"

"Something like jet lag, I should think," said Terry.

"That must be what Katherine was suffering from when I first saw her," I said.

David nodded. "It's said you feel it less when you get used to it. However, you can see that, one way and another, it takes both able and experienced researchers to carry out the far-back assignments."

"So they start by going to the twentieth century?" Terry asked.

"Yes, that's the nursery slope, so to speak. The twentieth century's supposed to be easy. If ever there was an age for ignorant skepticism, that's it. You could go into the twentieth century waving a banner saying I COME FROM THE FUTURE, and they still wouldn't suspect you. All they'd do is shake their heads and smile soothingly and send you to see a psychiatrist . . . The twentieth century is the last of the Middle Ages, as defined in our day. Do let me get you a drink."

David poured whiskey for Terry and my father. He looked rather wistfully at a third glass, but Margaret frowned, and he didn't give himself any. "Actually," he said, "I think it's the pubs that appeal to me more than the drink." Then he went on.

"The ideal research team," he said, "consists of two adults—one of each sex—and one or two young people. That way one gets different viewpoints on the same society, and different kinds of social interaction. Family groups, like ourselves, are strong candidates. But Margaret and Katherine and I are beginners. This is our first assignment, and the main thing we had to do was simply to get by unnoticed."

"Which we signally failed to do," said Margaret ruefully.

"There are other groups around, aren't there?" Terry asked.

"Yes. They're all on trial, like us. It's every historian's ambition to do a big assignment in the distant past. Even after those who can't time-shift at all have been weeded out, there's plenty of competition. There are four groups being tested in England at present, I think. They've all been sent to similar places at the same moment in time, to see who does well and who doesn't."

David paused. He'd been speaking fluently, and seemed actually to have been enjoying himself. But he looked tired.

"Old historic towns are best for time-shifting," he said. "The atmosphere's right, and you can always find places that haven't changed through the centuries, so you don't risk arriving in the middle of a brick wall. As you realized, Mr. Foster, there are other groups at Oxford and Durham at present. There's also a group in Edinburgh, I think, whose traces you don't seem to have found. Probably they'll win Sonia's approval; we certainly shan't."

Margaret winced at this.

"Sonia, as you may have guessed, is the head of our department," David told us. "Also our most accomplished time-shifter. Everything revolves around Sonia. Undoubtedly she's brilliant. Though I do rather wish she'd arranged for us to be better prepared."

"The minimal briefing is deliberate," Margaret said.

"I know, I know. The aim of the exercise is to test our resourcefulness and see how we cope with disorientation and the need for constant role playing. And so on and so on. It's a pretty grueling test, I can tell you . . . I wonder if it ever occurs to people like Sonia that we might get fed up with it all and go native."

"David!" protested Margaret.

"I don't dislike life in this time," David said. "I enjoyed the pub and the horse racing. And I'd like to drive an automobile, I think. A primitive but interesting way of getting around. Actually the thought of leaving so soon is rather a bore." David yawned. "I could almost be tempted to go native myself."

"David," said Margaret, "don't talk about going native. In fact don't talk any more at all. You've said much more than enough already. Go to bed."

"I *am* rather tired," David said. "A busy day. And I fear we are in for both a busy and a difficult time tomorrow. Perhaps if I may be excused I will retire."

This time nobody tried to stop him. When he'd left the room the remaining four of us looked at each other questioningly. Father had been sitting in stunned silence for the last few minutes. It was the first time I'd ever known him not to have anything to say. There was now a curious sense of mixed unreality and anticlimax.

Eventually it was Margaret who spóke. "You know," she said, "I am tired of the systematic lying, the posing and pretending, that we've had to do. I wish we'd never been involved with this project. Forgive me for saying so, but I feel we're contaminated by the worst of twentieth-century ways. Mr. Foster, what David was telling you was entirely the truth. Yes, we have come from 2149, and we shall soon be returning to it. I'm afraid that for Katherine it will be very painful. Apart from that, I shall be glad to go."

Father said, in a wondering tone of voice, "Do you know, I amost believe her. It's ridiculous, it's impossible, but I almost believe her."

"Oh, I believe her completely," Terry Foster said. "I have no doubt whatever."

"I believe her too," I said. I was thinking back to that first meeting on the Backs at King's. Yes, that had been just like an arrival. And when Alan saw a building that wasn't really there—hadn't it been an accidental sideslip into the future?

"I almost believe her," Father said. "But nevertheless, not quite. And in a matter like this, 'not quite' is pretty much the same as 'not at all.' No, I can't really swallow the 2149 business. There has to be a rational explanation of what's happened. And it has to be less bizarre than time travel."

"It's getting late," Margaret said, "and I must say I'm very tired too. I wonder if I might ask you now to leave me in peace?"

"Of course," Terry said. "I am so sorry."

"I don't know," said Father. "There's some funny

business going on, and the more I think of it the more I'm sure that we haven't got to the bottom of it yet." He turned to Terry. "How do we know they'll still be here in the morning?"

"I can promise you," said Margaret, "that we shall still be here tomorrow morning. I don't think we could get away while we're so tired. It will take joint concentration and a lot of effort go get back to our own time."

"I'm thinking of a more ordinary kind of disappearance," Father said. "It seems to me you're more likely to be fifty miles away than a hundred and fifty years away."

"Perhaps John would like to stay and be your watchdog," Margaret suggested. "He can sleep on the sofa here. There's spare bedding and he'll be quite comfortable. And if he moves the sofa in front of the door, he can at least be sure we don't run away to London during the night."

"A good idea," Father said, with surprising promptitude. "And, Terry, if you're feeling kind, perhaps you'll drive me home before you go back to the University Arms."

It struck me that Father would be glad to have the chance of a private talk with Terry. I'd never before seen him look so bewildered; he prided himself on knowing his own mind. As for me, I didn't mind being left behind in Park Parade. I had come to feel there was quite a strong bond between Margaret and myself. And Margaret was in lots of trouble, in what must seem to her to be a foreign land. I doubted whether David would be much comfort to her in a crisis.

fourteen

"You know, John," Margaret said, "you came to supper and you haven't had any."

"That's right," I said. "I'd forgotten all about it."

"I'll fix something for you now. I'm not hungry myself, and I don't propose to get David out of bed."

I never knew or cared what happened to the prepared meal, but Margaret gave me some bread and cold meat and salad. Finishing it, I said, "Margaret, there's so much more I still want to know."

Margaret said, "I may be able to tell you more tomorrow. I can't say anything tonight, I really can't. Good night, John dear. Sleep as well as you can."

"Oh, I shall sleep," I said. "I always do. And I know Mrs. McGuinness's sofa is comfortable. I've slept on it before."

I didn't however push the sofa across the doorway. I didn't believe the visitors would run away. And I remembered that Katherine was still out. I thought I'd probably be asleep when she came in, and I might take quite a bit of

145

waking. She wouldn't want to disturb the whole household.

But in fact I lay awake for a long time, going over and over the day's events, arguing round and round in circles about what I did and didn't believe, making different guesses about what Terry Foster and my father would do next. From somewhere in the city a clock struck, and seemed to go on striking at ever-shorter intervals. It was while I was trying to work out which clock it was that I fell asleep at last. Then I half woke again, and was dimly aware of Katherine, squeezing past the end of the sofa on her way in. And then I slept for a longer spell; but it was an uneasy, dream-crazed sleep, through which the visitors, my family, the McGuinnesses, Alan Stubbings, and Terry Foster moved in a kind of maypole dance of changing relationships.

Toward morning I had an impression that people were tiptoeing past me, but it was so confused with a variety of bizarre dream images that it didn't at first register sufficiently to wake me up. Then I began to have a sense of something amiss, a sense that this particular impression had been of a different order of reality from the dream material. And suddenly I was wide awake, and weak, dilute dawn light was seeping into the room round the window curtains.

I jumped up and put the light on. Not quite five o'clock. Without stopping to think whether it was a reasonable thing to do, I knocked hard on the door of David's and Margaret's room. No reply. No sound at all. I threw it open. And, as I'd known, there was no one there. I went to the next door—Katherine's—and repeated the process. She wasn't there either. I went back to the sitting

146

room, sat down on the edge of the sofa, and thought.

At first this seemed to turn the whole situation upside down again, to destroy my belief in the incredible. They'd flitted. It was quite simple after all. They were crooks and phonies, facing trouble for passing dud banknotes and, for all I knew, pursued by various other kinds of trouble as well. David's spectacular success at the track had nothing to do with knowing the future. How could it have? Either it was chance or, as my father suspected, there was skulduggery behind it somewhere, with horses drugged, switched, held back, or whatever might be involved in a racetrack coup.

Yes. Phonies. That's what they were. And how naive Terry Foster and I had been in believing this cock-and-bull business about Cambridge, 2149. Only my father had had his wits about him. What I should do now was obvious. Early as it was, it wasn't too soon for somebody to be getting on their trail. I should get to a phone booth as soon as possible, call my father and Terry, and tell them the birds had flown.

But I didn't. I stayed where I was. My reasoning on the matter was one thing, my feelings were another. Whatever they'd done, I didn't in fact want David and Margaret to be in trouble. In spite of everything I still had an instinctive sense that they were harmless and basically innocent. I still thought of them as friends—even Katherine, though she hadn't shown much interest in *me*. Perhaps it was really Ben I was thinking of rather than Katherine. I wasn't going to do anything that might land Ben's girl, or even her parents, in prison. In contrast, Father and Terry in their different ways were both successful people, and would go on being successful, whatever happened. They didn't stand to lose much if the Wyatts got away.

I decided I'd get back into bed and with any luck go to sleep again. In any case I wouldn't do anything before breakfast time. That would give them the best chance I reasonably could.

And then it struck me that I was jumping to conclusions. I went back to David's and Margaret's bedroom. There were small possessions on the dressing table. There were suitcases in a corner. I went next door, to Katherine's room. Clothes were hanging up. Her suitcase was there, too. If the Wyatts had fled, they'd fled almost empty-handed.

Of course, they might well have done that, though they risked leaving clues behind them. But . . . a further thought came to me. I opened the sideboard drawer into which I'd seen David stuff his winnings. And it was still crammed with banknotes. Genuine, used, no-risk banknotes. If they were crooks making their escape, would they really have gone and left all that money behind?

I was very thoughtful now. I switched off the light, drew back the curtains, and stood looking out over the pale, dawn-soaked expanse of Jesus Green, meditating. And then, under a tree, beyond the tennis courts, a little group of figures appeared. Literally they appeared. One instant they weren't there; the next instant they were.

I knew of course it was the visitors, though I couldn't distinguish faces at this distance and in this poor light. I went downstairs and out at the front door, noting that it was unlocked and on the latch. I crossed the street, went through the opening onto Jesus Green, and began to walk across the dewy grass.

Then the dizziness came over me. The tennis courts on my left, the band of trees across the green on my right, began to heave up and down, then slowly turned a full circle. I felt my legs giving way. Then I was half sitting, half kneeling on the grass, leaning to my left and holding myself off the ground with the palm of a hand. And the ground which I could feel through the flat of my hand was still turning, turning slowly round, so that the sky was underneath me and then on top again. And underneath and on top, and underneath and on top, faster and faster, and then I was unconscious.

Perhaps the unconsciousness lasted for seconds, perhaps minutes; I've never known. And then I was coming round, and not dizzy anymore, and the three of them were bending over me. And David and Margaret picked me up, my legs still weak, and walked me, arm in arm between them, back to Mrs. McGuinness's. By the time we got there I'd pretty well recovered, and went unaided up the stairs to their sitting room. I sat down yet again on the sofa. David sank into a chair opposite me. He and Margaret both looked gray and tired. Katherine pushed past both of us, as if to go to her room, then changed her mind and sat on the sofa, at the far end from me. She'd been crying. She was still crying.

"I'll put some coffee on for us all," Margaret said. "And we'd better keep quiet. I'd prefer not to wake the McGuinnesses."

"I don't need any more convincing," I said a minute or two later, sipping the hot, black, sweet stuff, "but please tell me what's going to happen now."

"All right," Margaret said. "I'll do my best. I don't think Sonia would approve. Perhaps that's why I didn't ask her. But you don't mind, do you, David?"

David shrugged his shoulders. "You're in charge," he said. "It's your responsibility. But I can't see that it makes much difference. It'll all be wiped out when we restore. Waste of breath, that's all."

"I think John might retain something," Margaret said. "Imaginative people sometimes do, for a time, or so we're told. He might remember a little about this—perhaps for long enough to see Ben through the parting."

"Parting?" I said.

Katherine was biting her lip, looking blankly out the window. It was daylight outside now. Inside, it was still dim, and faces were part shadowed. Across the river, lights were coming on in the upper floors of the tall houses along Chesterton Road.

"You mean . . ." I began.

"Yes," said Margaret. "It's the end of the road for Ben and Katherine. We have to go back."

"Back to . . . 2149?"

"Yes. As we expected. Experiment canceled."

"That happened this morning, didn't it? Out there on Jesus Green. I thought you'd vanished. I mean, vanished in the sense of run away. Well, you *had* vanished, hadn't you? Vanished literally. And while I was watching, you came back. Literally reappeared. It was a kind of vortex or whirlpool or something, a whirlpool of air, and I felt dizzy and frightened, as though if I'd gone any farther I'd have been sucked in. As Alan was, a few days ago."

"Yes. There's an instability."

"Of time. Or is it of space?"

"Of both, very briefly. At the point of intersection."

"I don't understand that."

"It doesn't matter, John," David said. "The fact is, we went back to consult Sonia. Our chief."

"As David did by himself on Tuesday," said Margaret, "when you wondered where he'd gone."

"And that didn't save the day," said David. "We've been recalled in disgrace. It's mainly my fault, I'm afraid."

"I'm responsible," said Margaret. "I'm the one in charge."

"Yes. And I know why Sonia put you in charge. It was because she didn't trust *me*. Anyway, to sum it up, you're responsible, I'm to blame, and Katherine is the one who suffers."

Katherine had got up and was standing in the bay window, looking blankly out over Jesus Green.

"She's in love," Margaret said. "You knew that, David. Of course you knew that."

"Go on, talk about me as if I weren't here!" Katherine said. "A departmental problem, that's all. Not a person."

"Katherine!" Margaret protested. "That's not like you!"

And indeed it wasn't. By our standards, relations between Katherine and her parents had seemed remarkably harmonious. But for once she sounded bitter. Margaret went over and tried to put an arm round her, but Katherine pushed her away.

"We *have* to talk about it," said David. "And, Kath dear, Margaret did well to get us a day's reprieve. We might have been told to drop everything and restore at once, without notice, just like that."

"A day's reprieve," said Katherine. "That's not much use."

"It's something," said Margaret. "And you took it."

"Of course I took it." Katherine was dry-eyed now but strained, getting wild in her manner. "Anything's better than nothing. But what I want is everything. Or rather, what I want is Ben, and never mind anything else."

"Kath, dear, we were warned about this," David said. " 'Don't get involved, don't make links you won't want to break.' How many times were you told that before you came?"

"I wasn't taking much notice," Katherine said. "I didn't think it could happen to me. And I suppose I just thought of the twentieth century as a period. I didn't think of it as being people like us."

"We are all liable to be sidetracked," said David. "Myself not least. And although I've been very self-denying about this stuff, I think I might now be allowed a small indulgence." He got out the whiskey bottle and a glass. And as he was pouring himself a drink, Katherine suddenly strode over, grabbed the bottle from his hand, and hurled it against the wall, aiming it deliberately at a large hanging mirror. There was a great crash of breaking glass. Fragments of bottle and mirror flew around. David picked a sliver of glass, calmly, out of his hair. Katherine rushed to the door, flung it wide, and was gone. We heard her footsteps thudding down the stairs, then the slam of the front door. David and Margaret stared at each other. And before anyone had time to speak, Mrs. McGuinness, in a bathrobe, was standing in the doorway.

"I was just coming down to make Mr. McGuinness's breakfast," she said, "and I heard the crash, and then that sound of somebody thundering downstairs. There's nothing wrong, I hope?"

She sniffed the air. There was a reek of whiskey.

"I hope the gentleman is all right," she said pointedly.

"I am perfectly all right, Mrs. McGuinness," David said.

"I'm glad to hear it," said Mrs. McGuinness, tight-lipped. "Such goings-on, and so early, too. Mr. McGuinness doesn't like this kind of thing at all. He was saying only yesterday, it can't go on like this, he was saying."

She paused for breath.

"I really don't see how you can expect to be allowed to stay," she went on. "Not that I'm a fussy person myself, but I have to think of Mr. McGuinness and his leg. And that mirror cost fifteen pounds, years ago, when things weren't so dear, and I don't know what I might have to pay now for another one like it."

"We shall see that any damage is made good," said Margaret with some dignity. "And now, Mrs. McGuinness, if you will be kind enough to lend me a broom and dustpan, I will clear up all this broken glass. I am very sorry about the disturbance."

"It's not that _I_ mind the disturbance . . ." Mrs. McGuinness began.

"No, of course, it's Mr. McGuinness," said David. "And his leg."

Mrs. McGuinness looked at him doubtfully, then went off to find a broom and dustpan.

"Margaret," said David, "what would happen if Katherine ran off and didn't answer her recall?"

"Don't be silly, David. Things are bad enough without these wild suggestions."

"She could, you know," David said.

"She couldn't. Of course she couldn't."

"Why not?"

153

"But one doesn't. It's absolutely ruled out. Katherine gave her undertaking, the way we all did. They won't let you go unless you sign the undertaking to come back."

"Undertakings can be broken."

"David, *please* stop being ridiculous."

"Well, you've read plenty of history. It's full of undertakings being broken."

"But that was long ago."

"We *are* long ago," said David. "We're in a time when people did break undertakings. Or should I say 'do'?"

"David," said Margaret, "you are being tiresome as well as absurd. For us to break an undertaking would be a breach of basic morality. It would be back to the bad old days with a vengeance. It's unthinkable!"

"It can't be unthinkable," said David. "We've thought it."

"Besides, I know Katherine," Margaret said. "She wouldn't. She couldn't, any more than I could."

"Don't be so sure," said David. "She might. And I'll tell you something else. If she did, I'd probably do the same. I could live quite happily in this time. It suits me very well. So much less orderly, less hygienic, less sober than ours. I'm not sure that a few months in this lively twentieth-century mess wouldn't be preferable to a lifetime of reliable good behavior in our own day."

"David!" Margaret sounded shocked. "I don't like to use such a word, but I think you're corrupted!"

"Would it matter?" I asked. "If somebody refused to go back?"

Both David and Margaret stared at me.

"What a question! Would it matter!" David said.

"David, he doesn't understand. It's elementary to us, it isn't elementary to him."

"All right," David said. "John, let me try to pick this up where Terry Foster dropped it last night. You realize that, as he was saying, everything you do now has its effect on the future? That is, the future is an endless web of consequences and interactions of all the things that happen, large and small?"

"Yes," I said. "Everybody knows that."

"Right. Now suppose that you're *in* the future and you send people into the past. Well, everything these people do will start putting new strands into the web of happenings. And it will work through into your own time. You can't tell what the result might be. It could be that the person you send into the past might talk to your own ten-times-great-grandfather and cause him to miss meeting your ten-times-great-grandmother, and then you wouldn't exist."

"Hey," I said, "that sounds like a dangerous game. Do you mean that everything *you're* doing now is changing your own time?"

"It would," David said. "Fortunately it's been found that the effect isn't instantaneous. It takes a while to work its way through, so to speak. The whole thing's governed by a very complicated equation which I don't pretend to understand. What it means in effect is that there's a safety margin before the effects of what we do here and now are felt in our own day. The time lag varies according to how far back you go—the further back you go, the longer the web takes to unravel—and for us in this particular case it's nearly a year. And during that time we can restore."

155

"Restore?"

"I mentioned restoration last night. It means putting things back as if nothing had happened. That's the technique that made time research a practical proposition. Once again, I don't claim to understand it. The scientific brains take care of it. There's some tricky physics and mathematics involved, but the upshot is simple. They cancel the whole affair. Nobody knows anything's happened. Nothing is changed. A stitch in time, you might call it."

"Nobody knows? You mean, if you go back and restore, *I'll* stop knowing about you?"

"Correct."

"Well, not absolutely," Margaret said. "To all intents and purposes, perhaps. But it seems there are a few people, specially imaginative or telepathic, who retain an impression for a while afterward. A kind of miragelike trace. It fades in the end, or maybe lingers as a ghost story. We've never heard of a case of permanent recollection, which is just as well, I suppose."

"And when you go back, will *you* forget about *me?*"

"Oh, no. That doesn't follow at all. What we're doing now will be part of our experience of life. Nobody's going to wipe that out. That's what makes it so hard for Katherine. When we restore, Ben will cease to know she ever existed. But she will remember him for as long as she lives."

"He's the lucky one," David said. "He won't know what he's lost."

"And of course, it anyone *did* remember," said Margaret, "they wouldn't be believed. That's the safeguard of all these operations."

"I'd have thought," I said, "that anyone coming from the future would be very special, immensely efficient. I mean, I don't want to be rude, but you're just like ordinary people."

"Having called yours an age of ignorant skepticism," said David, "we won't feel offended. Yes, we *are* ordinary people. At least, we're ordinary nonscientific academics. As I told you, this is supposed to be an easy assignment. We've been on trial here, and we've failed. And although the powers-that-be are a bit peevish about us, they don't think it really matters. We shall go back and restore, and that will be that."

"Actually," I said, "what I was asking was whether it would matter if somebody didn't go back."

"Well, yes," said David. "I'd have thought that was obvious."

"Even to an ignorant skeptic?" I asked.

"Pretty obvious. It's the one thing that could upset the applecart. How can we restore if there's somebody still wandering around changing things? *Everyone* has to be withdrawn from a time that's been visited before it can be put back as it was."

"I'd have thought that made the project risky," I said.

"Not very. Our society's not like yours. Agreements are observed. When people say they'll do something, they do it. When they say they won't do something, they don't do it. It's as simple as that."

"As simple and as sensible," said Margaret. "Frankly, I don't know how you manage with people breaking promises all over the place. It must make life very difficult."

"So," I said thoughtfully, "whatever happens, there's no future for Katherine and Ben?"

"There are futures for them separately. There is no future for them together. How can there be? They are not contemporaries."

"It's hard," I said.

"I find it hard to bear for them," said Margaret. "But you asked about this, and we've told you as much as we can."

Mrs. McGuinness put her head round the door.

"There's a young man to see you," she said. "The same as was here last night. Shall I send him up?"

Margaret nodded, a little wearily.

"That'll be Terry," I said. "Will you tell him what you've told me?"

"We shall tell him what we need to tell him. It depends on what we're asked."

"In that case," I said, "you can prepare to be busy. Terry won't be short of questions."

Margaret sighed.

"I suppose not," she said.

"Do you mind if I don't stay?" I asked, because suddenly I was feeling tired as well as overwhelmed.

"You must please yourself, John. You're not under any obligation."

"I think I am," I said, "but my obligations are going to take a bit of sorting out. In the meantime, I'm going home to breakfast."

"I'm a bit worried about Katherine," Margaret said. "If she's at your house, will you tell her so, and ask her to get in touch?"

I nodded. David looked at Margaret.

' You know," he said, "you told us that desertion was unthinkable, and I pointed out that we'd thought of it.

158

Well, once one begins to think the unthinkable, there's no telling where it will end. We agreed that if people were left around in the past, still changing things, there'd be drastic effects in our own day. And it's said that this can't happen, because we all give undertakings and abide by them. But are you sure, Margaret, that nobody's *ever* been tempted to break the undertaking, and given way?"

"I was told by Sonia personally that nobody, ever, has gone on living in the past."

"*Gone on living,*" said David. "O-ho. That's not the same as saying that nobody ever tried. I suspect, my dear, you're so accustomed to the sanctity of undertakings that you haven't noticed the difference. Remember what I was saying a few minutes ago? If there's *really* nothing to stop one from deserting, I might even try it myself. Or Katherine might."

"I rather think," said Margaret, "that Sonia has some means of persuasion she hasn't told us about. And now, please be sensible, David. Here comes Mr. Terry Foster."

fifteen

It was going to be one of those long, marvelous midsummer days. Dew on the grass, the air cool and icy-blue at this early hour, but wide open for the heat to come through later. Clear Cambridge light flowing full on the high creamy stone of churches and colleges, and in near-horizontal shafts that alternated with long-drawn shadows on streets and squares. Sunlight glinting on windows of little houses and just-opening shops, on the chrome of early cars and bicycles. The perpetual Cambridge contrast between the enduringly beautiful and the endearingly ordinary.

On this Thursday morning I walked homeward through the city with contradictory feelings: at the same time uplifted by the delight of a fine blue day and worried by the entanglements of my brother and my friends. I felt a little light-headed, too, from a night without much sleep.

No one seemed to be astir in our house except Sarah, who was sitting at the kitchen table eating cornflakes.

"Hello, minnow," I said.

160

"Hello, John."

"You're up early."

"I have been out in the garden," said Sarah. "Communing with nature. And talking to Katherine."

"Oh. So Katherine has been here."

"She is still here," Sarah said. "She got here an hour ago. She went straight to Ben's room. And Ben came down, and they went to get the dinghy. They were going up the river for the day. They took some food."

"But you say she's still here?"

"Yes. The dinghy has a puncture, and Ben couldn't find the repair kit. He's gone to get the Parfitts' boat, up by Newnham Pool. You know, that old boat they said we could borrow any time."

"And Katherine didn't go with him?"

"No. He wanted her to stay and talk to me while he brought the boat. He knew I would like that."

"Then why aren't you still talking to her?"

"We did talk for a time. Then she . . . didn't want to talk anymore. She didn't say so. I just knew." Sarah added solemnly, "I kissed her good-bye."

"That was a funny thing to do, minnow, when they're only going out for the day."

Sarah said nothing to that.

I wondered if I, too, ought to leave Katherine on her own. But as she was on the premises I couldn't neglect to tell her what Margaret had said. I went out into the garden.

Katherine was sitting under the copper beech, at a point where the lawn sloped sharply down toward the river. She was staring out across the water and didn't hear my approach over soft grass. I sat down beside her, and she turned toward me at last, but then turned away again without saying anything.

"Well?" I said after waiting a few seconds.

She was still silent.

"I've just come from Park Parade," I told her.

"I know."

"Your mother wants you to get in touch with her."

No reply.

"You could telephone her from here."

A pause. Then, "I don't think I want to speak to her. Not just now."

"I always thought you were very close to her."

"I always have been. And to David, too. But this is different. This is something that hasn't happened before. I'm not *ready* to talk to her. I only have today, John. You realize? Today, one day, is all I have."

I was on the point of telling her that David had spoken of desertion. Then I recalled that this was supposed to be unthinkable; and perhaps it really had been unthinkable so far as Katherine was concerned. In that case I had no business putting it into her mind. I stopped myself short. Instead I said, "You must have always known it had to end."

At last she looked me straight in the face. There was feeling as well as intelligence in the deep, dark eyes.

"Of course I did."

"And you didn't mind?"

"Of course I minded. But it was worth it. Shall I tell you something, John? I felt, and I still feel, that all my life so far was just leading up to Ben. And that all my life after this will just be life after Ben. What my life *is*, is now."

I remembered the serenity I'd noticed in Katherine after the day she and Ben spent together. And I remembered that she'd been willing to give the following morning to Sarah: a morning out of so few. I could have forgiven her a great deal for that.

"You *accepted* that that was how it had to be," I said.

"Yes, I accepted it. And I've been happy. I didn't know there *was* such happiness."

"But . . . was it fair to Ben?"

I knew Ben well. Maybe Katherine could settle for such brief happiness as there was, but whether it was possible for Ben was a different question. Ben would want permanence.

"It's not hurting Ben," she said. "You see, when it's all over, Ben will forget. I can hardly bear the thought of his forgetting, but that's what happens with restoration. He'll be unharmed. And while it lasts, John, Ben is happy. You know that, don't you?"

I did.

Katherine sighed.

"But I thought it would be at least a few weeks," she said. "Not just a few days. And today the last of them."

"Are you going to *tell* Ben?"

"I suppose I shouldn't. It could just be another long summer day with me, so far as he's concerned. But I think I will, all the same. I can't go through with it, saying nothing. He'd notice, and want to know what was wrong."

"And Ben has a strong character," I said.

"Yes. And . . . perhaps this is selfish, but I need to *know*, for sure, what Ben will tell me, knowing it's our last day. I need that to keep for the rest of my life. Whereas tomorrow it will all be over for him. Or should be."

"Here's Ben now," I said.

And indeed Ben was approaching, poling the Parfitts' boat—a beat-up and much-neglected old punt—toward our dock. He jumped ashore.

"A battered old thing," he said, "but at least it's dry. Better than the inflatable, really. Let's get those cushions from the shed, and we'll be off. Hello, John."

The last remark was no more than an aside. He'd hardly noticed me.

"Have a good day," I said to both of them. For a moment I felt the same impulse as Sarah, and wondered if I could kiss Katherine good-bye. But I was sure I'd see her again quite soon, so I didn't. Still, as I watched them piling cushions into the punt, more thoughts began to crowd in on me. When Ben knew it was his last day with Katherine—always supposing, of course, that he could believe it—would he just accept the fact? Why had Katherine said at the end that by tomorrow it would all be over, *or should be?* Though I carefully hadn't mentioned the possibility of desertion, could it really not have occurred to Katherine? Now I came to think of it, hadn't it lain unmentioned in the air between us all the time we'd been talking? And what had Margaret meant by implying that Sonia had other means of persuasion?

Should I try to intervene? Or should I mind my own business? I looked across once more at Ben and Katherine. They were kissing lightly; then Katherine stepped into the punt and Ben picked up the pole. And I knew I couldn't do anything more. Not now. Maybe I should, but I couldn't. Deeply troubled, I went back to the house.

* * *

164

As I arrived indoors, Father was just coming down the stairs. He was brisk and in good spirits.

"Well," he said, as he put bread in the toaster and coffee in the pot, "are the Whites still around?"

"Wyatts," I said. "Yes. They're still at Mrs. McGuinness's. All except Katherine."

"And where is Katherine?"

"She's gone up the river for the day with Ben."

"Oh." Father considered this. "A nuisance in a way," he said. "There are aspects of this affair that I'd like to discuss with Ben. But at least we know where they are, and presumably the Whites won't take off without Katherine. So one might say it helps to keep the situation under control."

He buttered a piece of toast.

"I wonder if those people are going to brazen the whole thing out," he said. "If so, I admire their nerve."

"You still think they're crooks, then?"

"I'm certain of it."

"Terry doesn't think so."

"Don't be so sure. Terry says he's keeping an open mind. I had a long talk with him after we left you last night. He says he'll consult the paper's experts about whether there are biochemical or other tests that would throw some light on our friends."

"The Wyatts may not want to be tested," I said. "And anyway, they told me this morning they have to go back to their own time in less than twenty-four hours. And they're going to restore. That is, put everything back as if nothing had happened."

"Oh, are they?" Father said. He asked several questions, which I answered as best I could. Then he shook his head.

"It won't wash," he said. "And if you ask me, Terry Foster's a good deal smarter than you might think from the way he seemed to be hooked on that wild theory. My guess is—" and Father smiled with satisfaction at his own acumen—"that Terry is letting them think he's on the wrong track while he accumulates evidence of what they're *really* up to."

"I *know* they're genuine," I said quietly, but Father took no notice.

"This tale of having to go back in twenty-four hours' time suggests to me," Father said, "that we must still be on the alert for a sudden disappearance. But the Whites must be very naive if they think we're going to assume they've vanished into the future. *I* shan't assume any such thing. Nor, I imagine, will the police. Or even, when it really comes to the point, Terry Foster . . . Do you want some coffee, John?"

"Yes, please."

"Pass your cup, then . . . All the same, the whole thing does raise some fascinating speculations. Suppose one really *could* go and find out about things that haven't happened yet. Think of the possibilities. Making a fortune would be child's play, of course, by means of betting or football pools or the Stock Exchange. But that's not all. Think of the advantages it would give to a historian. Or a journalist, of course. That won't have been lost on Terry. Imagine knowing for certain who's going to win the next general election, or be the next Prime Minister."

Father took another piece of toast.

"There might even be uses for such knowledge here in

Cambridge," he said. "Suppose one knew who was going to get the next professorial chair that became vacant. Or the next mastership of a college, even."

"Sounds alarming to me," I said.

"It's pure fantasy," said Father.

Laura wandered into the room, bathrobed and yawning. She was always the last to appear at breakfast time.

"What's pure fantasy?" she inquired.

"Knowledge of the future," said Father.

"Oh, I have a good deal of knowledge of the future," Laura said. "I predict, for instance, that in about fifteen seconds' time John will jump up in alarm, having been reminded that if he doesn't set out for school at once he'll be late for his exam."

"Wow!" I said. "I didn't realize it was so late. One up to you, Laura. Your prediction is fulfilled."

I had two exams that day, morning and afternoon, and it's just as well that they were in subjects I could have coped with in my sleep. Not that I was actually sleepy, though the day was hot and I hadn't had enough sleep the night before. It was just that I couldn't concentrate. I was there in body but my thoughts kept wandering away. Mostly I was speculating about the visitors, but from time to time I found myself moving in imagination up the cool shadowed river with Ben and Katherine. If they'd accepted the inevitability of Katherine's recall, they would be making the most of this last long summer day. They wouldn't be poling the dinghy through all these hours; they'd have tied up somewhere under the branches. They'd be in each other's arms; of course they would. For the first time, I found that thought acceptable.

When I got home at teatime, the house was oddly quiet. Father was spending the day at his college and hadn't got back yet. Laura was at an after-school staff meeting. There was no sign of Ben or Katherine. Only Sarah was around, and she was so small and silent you'd hardly notice her. She sat at the teak table under the copper beech tree, engaged on what looked like a complicated piece of tapestry.

I got myself a drink of cold milk, then took a book and sat in the garden. The river was busy, with craft of all kinds splashing past, and people singing tunefully or tunelessly and calling out in anxious or comically abusive voices. But the vessel I was looking and listening for, as I tried without much success to read, was the Parfitts' battered punt. Two or three times I thought I heard Ben's or Katherine's voice as a boat came round the corner from the mill, but I was mistaken every time.

As afternoon wore into evening, the river grew more peaceful. Voices were quieter and yet, in the curious way of voices across water, seemed to carry farther. It was a beautiful evening, and the air started cooling long before sundown, the lingering heat of high summer not yet established. Father and Laura arrived home in their separate cars at almost the same moment, and both raised their eyebrows when told that Ben and Katherine hadn't come back, but neither seemed unduly worried.

"It'll be a cold, salady kind of supper," Laura said, "so it won't matter what time they come in; there'll be nothing to spoil."

When the meal was ready, there were still only the four of us. Father had a book to review and was reading it at the table, fiercely, with occasional snorts of disagreement.

From time to time he made a rapid note on a scratch pad beside his plate. The charm was not switched on today. This was not unusual at family meals where no outsider was present. Sarah was at her most withdrawn, seeming hunched into an even smaller space than usual; and though she ate neatly and normally, she showed no sign of interest in her food. Once she met my eyes, and hers told me nothing.

As we left the supper table I asked her, "Did Katherine say anything to make you think she and Ben might not be back this evening?"

Her eyes were round and wide.

"No, John," she said.

"Then why did you kiss her good-bye?"

"I don't know, really. I just . . . thought I should. It came over me." Then, "John, has something happened to them?"

There were tears in her eyes now.

"Not that I know of," I said. "Don't cry, minnow. I'm sure they'll be all right."

Then the telephone rang. It was a call from a phone booth, and the caller seemed to be having a bit of difficulty. But eventually the voice came through. It was Margaret.

"I know what you're calling about," I said. "Well, Ben and Katherine set off upriver in a borrowed boat this morning, and they're not back yet. We were just talking about them when you called."

"I'm getting worried, John."

"It's only half-past eight, Margaret, and a fine evening."

"Still, Katherine knows we're recalled. And she went out in a temper this morning."

169

"I'm sure the temper's worn off. But they won't want to lose any of their last day by coming back early. And they can't actually have gone far, Margaret. There isn't all that far to go on this river." (That is, I said silently to myself, if they're still on the river.)

"I can't help feeling anxious, John. And that's not all. David went to the pub at lunchtime and persuaded a man to let him drive his car. And backed it into a wall."

"Oh, my God! Was he hurt?"

"No, but the car was. He gave the man money for the repair."

"Was David . . . fit to drive?"

"He wasn't drunk, if that's what you mean. I think he learned a lesson from his first hangover. But he's so irresponsible. Like a small boy, almost. There's no telling what he'll be up to next. He says that once we've restored it won't matter."

"From what you've told me," I said, "I suppose he's right."

At that moment the doorbell rang.

"But we can't restore until Katherine comes back," Margaret went on. "Oh, I do wish she would. We've only a few hours left. And I don't trust David at all."

The doorbell rang again. Why wasn't anyone answering it? I knew why, really. Father was in his study with the review book, and he didn't intend to let himself be interrupted. And I'd seen Laura go into the garden a minute or two ago with Sarah.

"Excuse me, Margaret," I said. "Don't hang up. I must just go to the door. Back in a minute."

There was a small grimy boy at the door with a note in his hand. It was addressed to "Mr. and Mrs. Hugh

170

Dunham." The writing was unmistakably Ben's. I gave the boy a coin, took the note, and unscrupulously opened it. It was just a scrawl of a few words. "Don't worry," it said. "We're both all right. Don't do anything until you hear from us. Will be in touch. This is all my doing. Love. Ben." And there was a postscript: "The boat is at Dead Man's Corner."

I went back to the telephone and read the note to Margaret. There was silence for a few seconds.

"Margaret! Are you still there?"

"Yes, John, I'm here. John . . . I'm not as surprised as I would have been a day or two ago, but . . ."

Her voice was shaky.

"But it's still a fearful shock. David and I will have to go forward at once and talk about this with Sonia. I'm dreading what she'll say. And I don't know what she'll *do,* but I know Ben and Katherine can't get away with it. That can't happen, it won't be *allowed* to happen. Oh, John, it's not that I *want* to separate them, but I can't tell you how relieved I'll be when this is over and the three of us are safely back in our own time!"

sixteen

The first time I tapped on the study door, there was no response. The second time, Father's voice said, "Go away." I opened the door all the same, and went in.

"Some day," Father said, "I hope you will improve your grasp of elementary English. I asked you to go away. Now you've diverted my train of thought. In fact you've shunted it straight into a siding."

I pushed Ben's note at him.

"I see you've saved me the trouble of opening it," he remarked. He read it through, twice, with a look of deepening irritation. Then he strode into the sitting room, calling for Laura. She appeared from the garden.

"Really," said Father, having given her a few seconds to read the note, "one's offspring can be an inordinate nuisance. In this day and age, a young man of twenty-one doesn't need to play Romeo. If he wants to get it on with a girl, what's stopping him? Surely they can be like anyone else of their generation and just *do* it, without making all this fuss."

"I don't think you understand Ben," said Laura. "Ben doesn't take things lightly. He has, if you'll forgive the old-fashioned phrase, a loving nature. He commits himself."

"I should hope," Father said, "that he doesn't commit himself too seriously on the strength of a week's acquaintance. People who go in too deep too soon are liable to make a mess of their lives."

"I like Katherine," Laura said. "And she and Ben do care for each other. There's something quite special between them."

"There's something quite ordinary between them," said Father. "Namely, difference of sex." He took the note, shoved it in his pocket, and left the room, muttering something about his interrupted review. Though he was irritated, I didn't think he was seriously concerned. But by breakfast time the next day he seemed to have given more thought to the matter, and was more disturbed.

"Ben," he said, "is a fool. An amiable fool, but a fool. It would be just like him to get into a hopeless tangle with this girl. And all we know about her is that her parents are total phonies."

"I know they're not phonies," I said.

"You're a fool as well," said Father. "But let me add to my previous description. Her parents are not only phonies, they're involved in forgery and probably in large-scale racetrack fraud. And heaven knows what else. I'll admit however that they are superb tall-story tellers, with a remarkable gift for making apparently intelligent people believe the most outrageous nonsense." He crunched a piece of toast challengingly. Nobody else spoke. Father went on, with a good deal of feeling, "Still, I repeat, Ben's a fool. The last thing any of us wants just now is to get involved with people of that kind."

"Hugh," said Laura, "do remember that Ben is sensible as well as considerate. He must have a reason for acting like this, and we shall hear it before long. Probably today."

"You're an incurable optimist," said Father. "And romantic as well. I only hope you're right. I didn't think there was anything in the note to suggest they were going to surface within the next few hours. And I must say, I could have done without such complications at this moment in my career."

"The mastership?" said Laura. "Oh, come off it, Hugh. It can't make any difference to that."

"I'm not so sure. Admittedly they're not going to say, 'We can't have a man as master of this college whose son runs off with a girl.' But involvement with dubious characters could be disastrous. In fact any kind of adverse publicity could swing the election against me. And although in a way I like Terry Foster, he's a journalist after all, and his first loyalty is to his paper. He could damage me if he chose to publish what he already knows about the Wyatts. The arrival from heaven knows where, the false identity, the banknotes, the racetrack winnings—can't you just see it as a Witness story?"

"Nobody could hold you responsible for the Wyatts," Laura said.

"No. But suppose the story included the daughter's disappearance with the elder son of the man most likely to be next master of a famous Cambridge college? Don't you think *that* might have its reverberations?"

"Terry wouldn't do that to us," I said.

"Maybe not," said Father. "I think Terry's after a bigger story than that. But if the bigger story is what *I* think it is, it'll be even worse. Or he could decide to print what he's got and pack the whole thing in. Besides, I'd have you remember—" he spoke in the tone of one who was putting us both morally in the wrong—"this is not merely a matter of adverse publicity, or even of the mastership. It's a matter of Ben's future. I suppose you realize that Ben is an extraordinarily brilliant physicist. He can't afford to damage *his* career."

"Now, now, Hugh," Laura said. "You know how devoted Ben is to his work. An episode like this won't make him throw everything away. All the same, I hope he gets in touch soon."

"There's nothing we can do about it if he doesn't," Father said. "The days of locking up daughters and threatening to cut sons off with a shilling are gone. Personally I rather regret it. At the moment I'd be quite inclined to cut Ben off with five pence, or even less. And now, I must be on my way. I've one hell of a day ahead of me. There's a meeting of trustees of that foundation of ours, and I shall have to do battle with entrenched stupidity. As if I didn't have enough of that already."

When Father had gone, Laura said thoughtfully, "You know, I feel sorry for Mrs. Wyatt. You told her about Ben's note, didn't you, John? It must be more worrying for her than it is for us. Even if there *is* something odd about the Wyatts."

"Margaret Wyatt's all right," I said. "I like her."

"I think I'll telephone her now," Laura said.

"You'll only get Mrs. McGuinness on the line, telling

you how bad it all is for Mr. McGuinness's leg," I said.

"I suppose so. And I haven't anything to say for Mrs. Wyatt's comfort, really. Perhaps I'd better leave it."

"I've no exams today," I said. "Why don't *I* go to Park Parade and rally round?"

"Why not?" said Laura.

Mrs. McGuinness, tight-lipped, opened the door to me.

"Well, John," she said, "I know you meant well, and you mustn't think I'm ungrateful."

My spirits sank further at once.

"But I've told the Wyatts definitely, they've got to go. It's too much for Mr. McGuinness. All that noise yesterday morning, when decent people were still in bed, and breaking my best mirror. Then the police coming round, making inquiries about some car accident. And then last night! That really was the last straw. Professor Wyatt was out in the street kissing and cuddling with that Billings girl who serves in the pub, and her no better than she should be if you ask me. Right out there in the street where everyone could see, if they happened to be looking out of their windows. My heart goes out to his poor wife. They'll have to leave!"

"I think they'll be gone in a day or two anyway," I said. "I'm very sorry, Mrs. McG."

"And I'm sorry too, John. I really am. But you see how it is."

"I'd better go and speak to them," I said.

I tapped on the door and pushed it open, a little apprehensive about what I might see. It could have been worse. David was lying on the sofa, and at least he was sober. He grinned sheepishly and said, "Hello."

Margaret came across and put her arms round me.

"John!" she said. "I'm so thankful you've come. Things are desperate, really desperate. We've defaulted on our agreement to return, so we're in trouble anyway. But that's the least of it. Our chiefs have run right out of patience with us. We've talked to Sonia, and the latest message is that any of us who don't go back by tomorrow night will be written off."

"Written off?"

"Abandoned. Left to our own devices. No return at all, ever."

"That's rough, isn't it? You mean, if Katherine doesn't show up by tomorrow night you might never see her again?"

"Oh, John, it's much worse that that! A person who's written off isn't left to *live* in the past, he's left to *die* in the past. We've been told all about it now. And now that we know, we understand why the authorities aren't worried about deserters. You see, actually it's quite dangerous for us to be around in your time at all. There are viruses and bacteria about for diseases that don't trouble us anymore. They've been stamped out. So we don't have the resistance to them that you have."

"I should have thought you'd be immunized," I said.

"Well, yes, we have all kinds of immunizations before we come. But there are so many strains of so many disease-causing bacteria and viruses, it just isn't possible to guard against them all. And some that have little or no effect on you can be fatal to us. John, if a person on a project like ours becomes ill, he or she will be recalled at once and treated, and isn't likely to come to real harm. But if people desert, they're on their own."

"So there have been some who've tried it?" I said.

"Yes, John. David was quite right when he said it wasn't unthinkable. It has happened. But nobody—nobody at all, ever—has deserted and survived. That's why they don't bother to send search parties. Anyone left around in the past will be hit within weeks or months by something against which he has no defense, and it will kill him. Our people know when this has happened, and then they can restore. It's not a problem for them—only for the runaway. Please understand, John. If Katherine stays behind, there is no hope for her, no hope at all. She must go back to her own time, or die."

"You *are* in trouble," I said. Then, "Would you go back without Katherine?"

"Oh, John, how *could* we?"

"But Katherine doesn't know about the danger," I said. "Not unless she gets in touch. Somehow she has to be found and told about it by tomorrow night. Is that correct?"

"Yes," said Margaret.

"Found, told about it, and persuaded to come back," said David.

"You need help. What about Terry Foster?"

"He's not around today. His paper transferred him to another story. They wanted something in a hurry for this week, and they thought he wasn't likely to get quick results here. He's hoping to be back in Cambridge tomorrow, or even tonight. But anyway, we couldn't expect him to set up a hunt for Katherine. And as for the police—can you imagine what your police would say if we told them the story?"

"Only too well," I said.

"So there's nothing we can do except wait and hope," Margaret said. "Hope that they get in touch before it's too late."

"It must be agony."

"It is agony. If only I could feel it was likely to come out right . . ."

"I don't believe in waiting and hoping," I said. "I'd like to go and look for them. Even if it *is* like looking for a needle in a haystack."

I was thinking hard as I said this. Actually it wasn't quite a needle-in-a-haystack search. Theoretically Ben and Katherine could be almost anywhere, but practically there were restrictions on their movements. So far as I knew, they had little or no money. They couldn't go abroad. They'd have to find somewhere to stay; and accommodation was expensive.

But it was university vacation time, and in university towns there would be a fair amount of student accommodation vacant. They wouldn't still be in Cambridge, that was for sure. The most likely place was Bristol, since Ben was at the university there. He'd probably have friends in Bristol with rooms or apartments he could borrow for a while. It wasn't a certainty by any means, but there was a pretty good chance one would find them in Bristol.

Of course, before I could look for them in Bristol I had to get to Bristol. But I had a solution in mind for this problem. I was thinking of Alan Stubbings's old car Theodosia.

It was still not much after nine. If Theodosia was in good form and Alan cooperative, we could get to Bristol by lunchtime or soon after.

"Let me see what I can do," I said.

179

seventeen

I cycled across the city to Alan Stubbings's house. He lived with his stepparents in one of the side streets off Mill Road, in Cambridge's east end. It was a modest row house, but well equipped and recently painted, the tiny front garden neat. Alan was in the kitchen eating a late breakfast, alone, with a textbook propped against the teapot. He greeted me with mild surprise and no great enthusiasm.

"What's up?" he demanded.

"Is your car on the road?" I asked him.

He took offense instantly.

"Of course she's on the road. You don't think I'd have a car that isn't serviceable? Theodosia's in first-class condition for her age. She'll go anywhere, any time."

"That's good. She can go to Bristol, then. And you as well. Right away."

"Go *where?*"

"To Bristol. Or have you something vital to do?"

"Plenty of studying. Vital but not gripping. But what would I be going to Bristol for?"

I took a deep breath and began. "When did you last see Terry Foster?"

"Last Tuesday. In Park Parade. While you were in the house."

"Did he tell you of a theory he had? About the Wyatts and where they come from?"

"Yes."

"Did you believe it?"

"If you want to know," said Alan, "yes." His tone of voice was brusque. He stared challengingly at me. Then he added, "If you'd had the experience I had, so would you."

"I believe it anyway. In fact they've admitted it."

He didn't say anything to that.

"And now they've been told to go back to their own time. But Katherine—the daughter—has gone off with my brother Ben." And I explained the danger the Wyatts were in, and why I thought Ben and Katherine might be in Bristol.

"Not my problem," Alan said. "I don't want anything more to do with those people."

"Then help me to get them out of the way and end all the fuss," I said.

Alan looked doubtful.

"Margaret's worried," I went on. "Desperately worried." I tried to explain the situation from her point of view. This had more effect on Alan. He'd met Margaret, and my guess was that he found her sympathetic, as I did.

Finally he said, "I might do it for *her*. I'm not interested in tracking down your errant brother. As a general proposition, I'd say that if Ben wants to make himself scarce it's his own business. He's got a right to go wherever he likes with whoever he likes."

"I go along with that," I said, "obviously. But . . ."

"Oh, all right," Alan said. "It sounds like a wild-goose chase, but not such a bore as the work I'm doing now. You can count me in. But remember, you're paying for the gas. And if we do find this couple, you promise you won't do anything except explain the position. I'm not taking part in any blackmail, or pulling any bourgeois chestnuts out of the fire."

"It's a deal," I said.

Alan seemed to like the idea of a trip to Bristol better as he got used to it.

"They'll be mad at me," he said, referring to his stepparents, "but there's nothing they can do about it. They can bawl me out, if they think it's worthwhile, but that's water off a duck's back. Come on, let's get Theodosia started."

In spite of Alan's boasts, the car wasn't too keen to start. The battery was weary, the engine slow to catch. But after a show of reluctance Theodosia cooperated in the end, and it wasn't many minutes before we were picking our way through narrow streets toward the London road. By eleven o'clock we were in the London area and heading westward. On the North Circular Road, where there were several delays, the water temperature went threateningly high, but once we were out on the highway and cruising in the Bristol direction Theodosia seemed more comfortable. A steady fifty miles an hour was within her powers, and although every time the slope of the road was against us there were signs of overheating, we got along well enough.

It was an overcast day, not in the least summery. I didn't mind that, but I did realize that the chances of success weren't high. There was also a possibility that sometime today Ben would telephone home and our journey would have been unnecessary. Oddly, though I desperately wanted Ben and Katherine to be found, that would have been the most infuriating thing of all.

We arrived in Bristol and had a hasty coffee-bar snack. Then we set off, following our only clue, which was that I knew the address of the flat Ben shared with two friends in Clifton, a Bristol suburb. The result was an immediate blank. No response to the doorbell. It could just be of course that someone was there and not answering, but I pushed open the mail slot, declared my identity, and bawled in succession Ben's name and those of his two friends. I was sure that if there'd been anyone in they'd have answered me. There was nobody at home.

Too bad, but not altogether unexpected. I'd compiled a mental list of those of Ben's friends whom I'd met or heard of. We sputtered up and down the sloping streets of Clifton and Redland, called in at the residence hall where Ben had lived in an earlier year and at the university administrative office, and still drew nothing but blanks. There was no sign of Ben, or of any of his friends. With the onset of the long vacation, it seemed that everyone who knew him had disappeared to the ends of the earth.

Alan began to make impatient noises after the fourth fruitless visit. But on the fifth we found a slim clue, when the landlord of a seedy rooming house told us we might find one John Bold, mentioned by Ben from time to time, at another house just round the corner.

"He moved from here last month without paying his rent," the landlord said, "and in spite of losing the money I wasn't sorry to see him go."

On the next street, in an attic room in an even seedier house, we found John Bold, a large, ginger-bearded young man, just getting out of bed in midafternoon.

"Ben?" he said, and shook his head, then screwed up his face in agony at the effects of the head-shake. "I had a rough night last night," he explained. "As for Ben, no, I haven't seen him for weeks. Not since that girl's party."

We waited. John Bold went out to the tap on the landing, brought back a jug of water, drank a large mugful, poured the rest into a basin, and prepared to wash his face. Then he said, "I suppose you could try speaking to her. Her name's Elaine Something-or-other. Lives with her parents at Westbury and reads the same subject as Ben. Rather a prissy type, I thought, but Ben seemed to tolerate her. She's the only girl I remember him going out with, as a matter of fact. He's never been one for the women."

This seemed to be the full extent of John Bold's information. With an effort of concentration, he eventually remembered Elaine's surname. We left him toweling his face and groaning about the state of his head.

A call to Westbury, more successful than most of our inquiries, brought Elaine to the telephone. She had a clear, high, rather little-girlish voice, and didn't sound like the type I'd have associated with advanced science, but perhaps that was just a bit of bad old sexism on my part. She was interested at once when I told her I was Ben's brother, and I could hear the disappointment in her voice

184

when I explained that I had nothing to tell her about Ben and in fact was trying to trace him.

"I only knew he'd gone to Cambridge for a few days," she said. That seemed to take us full circle. But then at last came a real clue. "He talked at one time of cruising for a week or two, later this summer, on Harold Thompson's canalboat."

"Harold Thompson?" I'd heard the name but couldn't immediately place it.

"He's a lecturer in our department."

"Oh yes, of course. I remember now. Ben's mentioned him once or twice."

"Harold only started here this year. But he and Ben have become buddies."

Somehow I hadn't thought of a lecturer as a likely contact, but Elaine went on. "He's only twenty-five, after all. Took his doctorate last year. Very brilliant."

"Like Ben," I said.

"I don't know whether he's as brilliant as Ben, but he's certainly brilliant. He lives in Manchester somewhere. Hold on, I think I can find his home number."

She was away for some time. I put more coins in the slot. Elaine came back with the number. Then she asked me several questions about Ben, which I parried. "Ask him to call me as soon as he can," she said finally. There was a wistful note in her voice.

I tried the Manchester number at once, but my luck with the telephone had run out for the time being. There was no reply.

"I told you it was all a wild-goose chase," Alan said. "Let's have a bite to eat and set off home."

"We'll have a bite to eat," I said. "I don't know about setting off home."

"Well, have you anything to work on? Looks to me as though we're at a dead end until we get hold of this Thompson chap. And seeing he's in Manchester, we don't gain anything by staying in Bristol."

That seemed reasonable enough. I had in fact no other clues whatever. We had sandwiches at another snack bar. Then I called home. Laura was back from her day's teaching, and it was all too evident from her voice that she'd hoped it might be Ben on the phone. Her disappointment was followed by surprise and concern when I told her where I was. I prevented long discussion by saying I hadn't any more coins, and by carefully failing to hear her when she proposed calling me back.

We left for home, but some impulse made me urge the cross-country route, which would take us from Bristol to Cambridge through a long string of villages and small towns, rather than the highway. Alan agreed; he didn't mind a change. But he wasn't too pleased when, after we'd been an hour on the way, I wanted to stop at a telephone booth. He sat impatiently in the car while I tried once more for the Manchester number. When I came back to him he was sullen but I was unexpectedly hopeful.

"Did you ever hear of a place called Dutton, in Cheshire?" I asked him.

"Never."

"Well, you've heard of it now. Get out the road map. We're going there."

"Oh, are we? Why?"

"I've spoken to Harold Thompson. And you remember that Elaine said he had a canalboat? Well, Dutton is where it's tied up. And Harold Thompson says Ben doesn't merely know about the boat, he knows where to find a key, and has permission to use it. Well now, if you wanted to lose yourself in England with a girl, can you think of anything better than a canalboat?''

"You're just guessing," Alan said. But I know Alan well, and I knew what would happen next. He'd argue about it a bit, but he'd go.

And he did go. Dutton, we found, was at the northern-most end of the Trent and Mersey Canal, which runs from the English Midlands toward the northwest. It was mid-evening when we got there: a cool, silvery-gray evening. Theodosia, running sweetly and giving Alan great satisfac-tion, had taken us for some miles through a pitted and scarred industrial landscape; but now that lay behind us and we were in a stretch of deep country. The canal, still as a mirror, reflected a white sky, and deep-green trees grew downward through the water. A quarter-mile away was the black, half-round, absurdly small entrance to a tunnel; a narrow lane ran down to it from the main road, and there was room to park a car.

On the opposite bank from the towpath a line of boats was moored: long, high-tillered narrow-boats painted with diamond and lozenge patterns, roses, and castles; sleek streamlined cruisers in white and colored fiberglass and varnished mahogany; humbler wooden craft that had known better days and now seemed held together by love and hope. Only the blows of a hammer, sharp as pistol shots against the silence, broke the evening's peace.

This beyond doubt was where Harold Thompson had told me his boat was moored. We walked up and down the

187

towpath, the length of the line. There was no sign of a narrow-boat called *Tarantella*, but there were three or four gaps where she might formerly have been. The hammering came from a lean, cheerful-looking young man who seemed to be building his own superstructure onto a narrow-boat hull. I shouted across to him.

"*Tarantella?*" he said. "Sure. That's Harold Thompson's boat. Her mooring's next-door-but-one to mine. There's a board with her name on it, but it's so small you probably can't read it from that side of the cut."

"Do you know where she is?"

"She left here yesterday. Harold's friend was on board. I can't remember his name."

"Ben?"

"That's right. Ben."

"Was there a girl with him?"

"Why do you want to know that?" The young man was suddenly suspicious.

"It's my brother and his girl friend," I said. "We need to find them. Family business, very urgent."

He hesitated. Then he grinned doubtfully and said, "Well, you have an honest face, what little I can see of it. I can't tell you much anyway. They were here and now they aren't. They set off yesterday afternoon through the tunnel. Didn't say where they were going, but they must be on the Bridgewater. Probably they're in Manchester by now. Or somewhere between here and there. They can't have gone over to the Leeds and Liverpool, because the swing aqueduct's being repaired."

"How could we go after them?"

"You could swim. Or walk along the towpath . . ."

"Can't we hire a boat?"

"Well, you could try. You won't get one here. There's a boatyard a few miles back, but they're probably fully booked at this time of year."

"What if we . . . ?"

"You're wearing my voice out. Anyway, I must get on with this job while there's still light. I'll wish you luck." And the hammerblows were restarted.

"Well," I said to Alan, "we're getting somewhere. "

"I suppose so. I feel as if the whole thing had lost touch with reality. And I'm tired. What do you propose now?"

"I propose," I said, "to call Margaret Wyatt and tell her how far we've got."

"And what about our parents?"

"We'll just tell them we're all right. I don't want to bring my father into this at present. I don't quite trust him. But I have to tell Margaret. It's her problem, and she was going wild with worry."

"All right. You're paying the piper, I suppose you can call the tune. And talking of paying the piper, which four-star hotel are we staying at tonight?"

"To hell with four-star hotels," I said. "We're sleeping in the car, right where it is. There was a phone booth in the village. I'll do the telephoning while you drive on to the boatyard and see if there's anything for hire. It's no good looking for a canalboat by car; there are too many places where it could tie up out of sight from any road and we'd never see it."

"Aye, aye, sir," said Alan sardonically; but at least he didn't tell me to get stuffed. The telephone calls took me less than ten minutes. Then I was standing around, waiting for him to come back. For a June evening it was none too warm. I walked up and down for a while, shivering, wondering whether Alan had managed to have an accident in the short distance he had to drive, or whether poor old Theodosia, surprisingly docile all day, had decided at last that she'd done enough. But finally Alan reappeared, driving quite fast and pulling up with a squeal of tires.

"Any luck?" we asked each other simultaneously. Then Alan said, "Go on. You go first."

"Well, I told our families. Mine took it quite well, all things considered. They still haven't heard from Ben. Laura wished us luck. I'm afraid *your* stepmother got obstreperous, though. I had to hang up on her in the end."

"You did right," said Alan. "Silly old cow. It's not as if she cared what I do, it's just that she wants her finger in the pie. Interference without interest, that's her style."

"Anyone'd think you didn't like her."

"No comment. Still, I'm glad it was you, not me, that spoke to her. I'd probably have got into a shouting match. What about the Wyatts?"

"I talked to Margaret. And then to Terry Foster."

"Ho hum. So he was around. Whose side is he on?"

"He says he's on theirs. And Margaret thinks he is. And listen, Alan, things are getting desperate. Margaret's at her wits' end with fright about what will happen to them, especially of course to Katherine. Alan, they've got to find Katherine soon. Or we have."

"You mean they're leaving it to us?"

"No. Terry's driving David and Margaret up here overnight. I told him where to find us."

"Do you trust Terry, John?"

"What else can we do?" I said. "I guess we *have* to trust him."

190

"Oh well," said Alan. "We have another reason for needing adults around. The boatyard thought at first they hadn't anything, then they produced a weird-looking vessel we can rent from tomorrow morning. But the renter has to be twenty-one or over. And they didn't seem to think I was twenty-one. So this is where either the adults come in or I bow out. And I don't really want to bow out. Not at this stage."

"You'll see it through, then?"

"I expect so. Stupid of me, letting you lead me off on a caper like this. But I want to know what happens. Yes, I'll see it through."

eighteen

I don't know how we'd have managed if none of us had known how to handle a canalboat. But the moment David Wyatt set eyes on the horrible thing that was all the boatyard could find for us, he was suddenly and delightedly in his element.

"It's an icebreaker!" he declared. "A genuine icebreaker, none of your reproductions! Just look at it! Isn't it a gem? A real, honest-to-goodness, original, working icebreaker!"

"Does it matter *what* it is, David, as long as it goes?" said Margaret.

"Goes all right," said the boatyard man. We all stood back and let him show an ecstatic David the controls. The boat was very narrow, and short compared to the ones we'd seen the day before. It was battered and peeling, but the iron hull, heavily ribbed and studded with rusty rivets, looked solid enough. A cabin had been built in front of the engine room, with bunks and a battered stove and lockers, but we were in such a hurry to be off that we didn't stop to learn how everything worked. The boat was steered from the back with a long tiller, and the moment the engine was started David stood up there and edged us out into mid-channel, as if he'd been doing it all his life.

There was a tranquil stretch of canal, winding round open hillsides with views of a broad valley to the left, then a gloomy length of green water overhung by trees, and then suddenly a brick arch round a black hole: the tunnel that Alan and I had seen the previous evening.

"This is a tricky one," said David cheerfully. "Twists about, and there isn't room to pass in it."

"How does he come to know so much about it?" I asked Margaret.

"Canals are one of David's enthusiasms," Margaret said. "One of his more harmless enthusiasms." She smiled thinly.

Beside the tunnel mouth, confirming what David had said, was a sign restricting the hours for northbound and southbound traffic: two hours at a time, turn and turn about. We were northbound, with an hour and a half of southbound traffic to go before it was our turn.

"Risk it," said Terry.

"Hmmm . . ." said David doubtfully, but after one look at Margaret's drawn face he changed his mind. "John," he said. "Somewhere inside there'll be a switch for a headlight. Find it and put it on."

Then suddenly we were engulfed by darkness, and by the throbbing noise of our own engine thrown back off the walls and resounding down the space ahead. I went and stood in the front cockpit of the boat. There was no end to the tunnel in sight, not even a pinpoint of daylight in the distance; and for a horrible moment I fought down a sick feeling that we were going into the bowels of the earth forever, and would never get out. The boat's headlight showed a dim red oval ahead—the endlessly arching wet brick walls of the tunnel reflected in the black water. Occasional drips from above fell coldly on my face.

The walls snaked about, and David had trouble steering; several times we ground along the brickwork at one side or the other. And I began to take the measure of that doubtful "Hmmm." What would we do if we met an oncoming boat? Could one back up? I didn't know. There wouldn't be room to pass, that was for sure. I shuddered, went inside, and found a kettle to make tea. I thought we could do with it. And we were still chugging through the gloom when I had made and poured tea, and drunk my own. Margaret sat on one of the bunks, sipping hers and saying nothing. Alan and Terry stayed outside at the back with David, who whistled the tune of his song about the ladies of the port.

I joined them. We were in sight of the end now. Ahead of us, though still some distance away, was a greenish translucent oval, half daylight, half reflection. Light gleamed along the roof and walls toward us, on twisting rows of brick. We couldn't see the waterline, and appeared to be eerily suspended, gliding in midair with nothing to support us, between the arc above and the arc below.

Suddenly the lower arc wavered and broke. A blinding star shone at us; below it the dark outline of a boat. A southbound craft had entered the tunnel, coming toward us. At once it hooted, long and angrily. David found our horn and we boomed back—a mournful, hollow reverberation. The engine note dropped as we reduced speed. At first the other boat came on, but David kept going, slowly

194

and steadily, sounding his horn two or three more times. Then the other boat went into reverse and began to back out ahead of us.

Margaret came out of the cabin. "What's happening?" she asked. "Why are we going so slowly?"

Terry told her. She groaned.

Then we were out in the suddenly bright, suddenly warm air, with the tunnel behind us. The man at the tiller of the boat we'd driven back was waiting for us, furious. He began to shout.

"Sorry, sorry!" called David, putting on speed and sweeping past him.

"You bloody well stop and explain yourself!" yelled the man.

"No time!" called David.

"Whose right of way d'you think it was?"

"Yours!"

"What if we'd met in the middle?" bellowed the voice, now some distance behind us.

"What indeed?" replied David, waving.

Just for once I felt grateful to the devil-may-care fellow that Professor David Wyatt so readily became.

Margaret was alarmed by the encounter. "What if that man comes after us and stops us?" she said. "Oh, David, do *hurry!*"

"He can't do that," said David lightly. "And we can't go any faster. I'm doing ten miles an hour already, and the speed limit's four."

"But it's so slow!" Margaret's control was beginning to give way. I could see she was on the edge of tears. "David, you must stop fooling around and get us there. Have you forgotten, it's a matter of life and death?"

David suddenly put aside his air of wild cheerfulness and said firmly, "Margaret, dear. You're always the calm one, remember? Now, listen. That cross gentleman can't come after us because his boat is seventy-two feet long. Right?"

"I don't see it," muttered Alan.

"That's longer than the canal is wide. He needs a winding hole to turn in, and there isn't one for miles the way he's facing. So don't worry about him. As for speed—well, this is a lovely canal, wide and straight and deep, and we're going to go as fast as any boat could ever go. And sometime today we shall catch up with Ben and Katherine. I promise you."

"Why don't you lie down and rest?" suggested Terry.

Margaret nodded. "Perhaps I will. If we—when we find them, I shall need to have my wits about me. It still won't be easy."

So Margaret slept. Alan and David took turns steering. Terry and I sat on the cabin roof, looking out all the time for a boat called *Tarantella:* she might, of course, have been tied up anywhere. And we watched the landscape flowing past. It was surprising how quickly one got used to slow canal speeds. When, later, a road came close alongside the towpath, I was amazed by the reckless pace of the cars: I thought at first the drivers had gone mad, then realized how snail-like was our wild pursuit. Yet it *did* matter. Life and death, Margaret had said; and ours was the only way.

But a sense of unreality gradually took possession of me. It was partly the strange sensation of traveling almost entirely out of sight and sound of any road. Little had changed about the canal since it was built; I wondered if I

196

too was on a journey in the past. And it was curious to be so lost in this world whereas David, whose own time was far away, was so much at home and so knowledgeable. He kept pointing things out to us—grooves worn by towropes in the undersides of bridges, for instance—and telling us about them.

By early afternoon we were on the outskirts of Manchester. At least the sight of town reminded us which century we were in. Rows of houses abutted on the canal at one side; electric trains flashed along the railway line at the other. An engineer hooted a greeting to us. On a wide grass verge by the water children played and an occasional angler sat unmoving. There were a few boats tied up, some of them shabby or even half-submerged; none was called *Tarantella*.

We chugged steadily on, farther and farther into the grimy backyard of the city. Now we moved in a broad deep ditch below more and more ugly bridges, past factories and warehouses. Once or twice we passed wharves where huge barges were tied up and appeared to be rotting away. Muck and debris floated in the water.

David became gloomy. "It looks so *old*," he said.

"It *is* old," Terry reminded him. "About two hundred years."

"Yes, but it looks older than it *will* be," said David, shaking his head.

We passed under a huge web of road and rail bridges, then worked our way round a bend. On our right a cindery towpath edged the cut. A remnant of bridge, as narrow as the path itself, clung to a wall under which was a bricked-in arch, where once an arm of canal must have led to some wharf or warehouse. Beyond it, the cindery path contin-

197

ued. And tied up beside it was a single long narrow-boat. *Tarantella.*

I slipped into the cabin, and gently shook Margaret awake.

We tied up the icebreaker a few yards behind the narrow-boat and walked along the towpath. *Tarantella* was a loved and cared-for boat with bright, fresh paintwork, well-scrubbed decks, and over her rear cabin a small chimney with three polished brass rings round it. No doubt she was Harold Thompson's pride and joy. But the elation of spotting her died down rapidly. I felt an extreme shyness, even a fear of what I might find. Although I thought I'd conquered my jealousy, I wasn't sure I was equal to encountering Ben and Katherine as lovers.

The doors and windows of the boat were all closed, and the curtains on the landward side were drawn. It was probable that there was nobody on board. Probable, but not certain. The five of us looked at each other, all hesitating. Then Terry stepped forward and made as if to jump from the towpath into the front cockpit of the boat. I frowned and waved at him, and he drew back.

"I'm going to whistle," I said. "A tune Ben and I used to whistle as a signal to each other when we were little. If he hears this, he'll know it's me." And I whistled, piercingly, the tune of an old song, "If I Were a Blackbird." My whistle was loud enough to echo from a wall at the other side of the canal. But there was no response.

"Might as well knock now," Terry said, and I didn't argue with him. He jumped on board and beat a tattoo on the front door. Still there was no reply. I was convinced by now that there wasn't anyone on board, and I didn't object when I saw Terry Foster edging his way along the catwalk, peering in as best he could at each window. I knew that another dark possibility was in his mind; it had occurred to me, too.

"I think they've gone," Terry said at last. "I hope they haven't left the boat for good. Perhaps they're just shopping and will be back soon. Why don't we have some lunch?"

It was midafternoon now, and none of us had eaten. We had a little basic food, picked up in haste that morning, and we made some kind of a meal; I hardly noticed what it was. The day was fine and had become hot. The sun shone hard down into the canyon formed by high buildings on either side of the canal. Bits of driftwood, plastic squeeze bottles, and squares of styrofoam floated on the canal's opaque surface. No vessels came past. A couple of small boys arrived and began to fish, unconvincingly, from the towpath. I couldn't imagine what they expected to catch.

Nobody came to *Tarantella*.

At half-past four I said, "I'd better call Harold Thompson." A quarter-mile away, a bridge over the canal carried a busy urban road. Beside it was a telephone booth. I dialed. A rather thin male voice with a pronounced northern accent answered.

"Can I speak to Harold Thompson?" I asked.

"You're speaking to him. Who is it?"

"John Dunham. Ben Dunham's brother."

"Oh." A pause. "What can I do for you?"

"It's about Ben."

"I thought it would be. Well, what about him?"

"We traced your narrow-boat. It's tied up on the canal, well in toward the center of Manchester by the look of it."

199

I described the setting. "Ben was on it, we were told, and this girl. But they're not on board now. I wonder if you know where they are."

There was a silence of several seconds. I said "Hello?" anxiously, wondering if we'd been cut off. Then Harold said, "I'm a bit worried about this. For all I know, Ben may not want to see you. I can't see that it's up to me to help you find him."

"It's very urgent family business," I told him.

"Yes. I think I know what it is. But Ben isn't a child, he knows what he's doing. When he thinks it's time to get in touch with his family, he'll do so."

"But there's a factor in the situation," I said, "that Ben doesn't know about. Or his—his girl friend either. She's in danger and she doesn't realize."

"What sort of danger?" asked Harold. It was a reasonable question, but impossible to answer in any way that would carry conviction.

"I . . . can't really tell you," I said. "I can only say it's genuine. Absolutely genuine. I swear it."

There was another silence. Then Harold said, "Stay by the boat. I'll come and see you."

I had to be content with that. I went back to our boat. It was as hot as ever and the little cabin was stifling, but it wasn't any better outside; there was no protection yet from the sun. I reported progress.

Alan was cross and impatient. "What I want to know," he said, "is how and when I shall get back to my car."

I couldn't answer that one. And I was thinking more about the adults on board. David was restless and obviously chafing at the inactivity. Margaret was wound up, tense as a spring. Whenever I caught her eye, she smiled mechanically. But I knew she was suffering more than any of us.

Terry's manner, as always, was relaxed, but I sensed anxiety in him, too. Once or twice he walked along the towpath to Harold's boat, surveyed it thoughtfully, and walked back again. I knew what he had in mind. Katherine would certainly have told Ben of her recall. The same dark possibility as before was troubling Terry. He would have liked to see inside that boat. I felt that if Harold didn't come before long he would be tempted to break in.

And we waited what seemed an eternity for any sign of Harold. By our watches it was late afternoon, then early evening, but the sun seemed to have got stuck in the sky, and stale heat lapped the canal. Terry made some instant coffee. We had no milk, and everyone drank it black. It was not refreshing.

When Harold appeared at last, however, striding toward us along the towpath from the city center, I had no doubt that this was our man. In an odd way, his appearance fitted his voice. He was tall, thin, and angular. He had curly, unkempt blond hair and a blond moustache that straggled out to meet it; and he wore round-lensed, gold-rimmed spectacles. He neither smiled nor greeted us.

"Well," he said, "I've seen Ben. And Katherine."

"And are they all right?" Margaret asked anxiously.

"They're all right. And willing to see you. Or at any rate, prepared to see you. I'm going to take you to them now."

nineteen

We followed Harold back along the towpath, the way he'd come. Buildings continued to loom over the canal for most of the way. There were walls in every state of repair, disused hoists and docks, bricked-in archways, faded names of firms painted on peeling gates; everywhere moss and grass and lichen, and flowering weeds rooted improbably in ancient brickwork. At length we came to a bare cindery site, sloping upward from the canal toward a big new slabby housing development. In the foreground, almost on the canal bank, was a derelict building, the size of a short row of cottages. In its gable end at second-floor level was a door, obviously once used for some long-forgotten canal purpose, now opening onto nothing.

"Can you climb?" Harold asked; but he didn't wait for an answer. With the help of toeholds provided by missing or broken bricks, he scrambled up a drainpipe, then leaned far over to tap on the gable-end door. It opened, and an arm helped him in. A few seconds later the door opened again, and Harold pushed out a ladder, the end of which slid quickly to the ground. We all went up it except

Alan, who preferred Harold's route up the drainpipe.

Going inside from the bright sunshine, you couldn't see much at first. Then you realized you were in a long, low attic. Only in the middle could a grown person stand upright. Three small grimy windows in the sloping roof, all now pushed wide open, let in a little light and a little air, but none too much of either. There was a camp bed, a couple of rugs, a pair of battered armchairs, a paraffin stove. And there were Ben and Katherine, sitting side by side on the camp bed.

"Well?" said Ben.

Nobody spoke at first. Margaret went across to Katherine and embraced her. They held each other tightly, both on the brink of tears.

"Well?" said Ben again; then, "All right. I know. She's told me everything."

"She can't have told you everything," Margaret said. "I'm afraid she didn't *know* everything." She went on. "Katherine, because you'd gone, we didn't answer our recall on Thursday. We've been given an extension until tonight. Any of us who haven't gone back by then will be written off."

"What does that mean?" Ben asked.

"Left behind in the past," said Margaret. "When people are written off, they're discarded from the system and never heard of again."

"But they're still alive in *our* time?" asked Ben. There was sudden hope in his eyes. Katherine released her mother and took his hand.

"If that's possible," she said, "I shall stay. I'm sorry if it hurts you, but I shall." There was a new, determined note in her voice that hadn't been there two days ago.

"It isn't possible," said Margaret. "There are still things you don't know. First, when people are once written off they stay written off. They can't change their minds later."

"That's all right," Katherine said steadily. "I accept that the choice is final. It's my life, and I am ready to be discarded."

"Don't speak too soon," David said.

"There's a snag, isn't there?" said Ben quietly.

"Yes," said Margaret, "there is. Katherine dear, people have been written off before. Do you know what the one-year survival rate is?"

"I haven't any idea."

"It's nil, Katherine. I checked with Sonia. About thirty people have been left at various points in the past. The longest any of them ever survived was nine months, and that was a freak. The average isn't much over three."

"What did they die of?" Ben asked.

"Two were killed in accidents and one committed suicide. The rest all died of virus or bacterial diseases. Unless she has an accident first, that's what will happen to Katherine if she stays. There are several that could kill her, and one or another of them certainly will."

"Give me an example," Ben said.

"Well . . . it's not a nice task. How do you like the thought of meningitis?"

"Not at all. It's nasty."

"It could well be what she would die of. Meningococcus bacteria are widely carried in your day but not in ours. Katherine doesn't have your resistance to them. After a cold, for instance, she would be extremely likely to get meningitis, and extremely unlikely to survive it."

"What if I caught something like that *now?*" Katherine asked.

"You'd be all right, because you haven't been written off. You'd be recalled at once and treated. But if you were here on your own, a deserter . . . my dear, there would not be a hope."

"Very well," Katherine said. "I shall stay without hope for as long as I live. It will be worth it."

But Ben turned on her in outrage.

"You won't be so absurd!" he said. "You're not giving up the rest of your life for a few weeks or months."

"I am," said Katherine. She sounded calm now; calm and determined.

"Margaret," I said, "are you sure about this? I mean, are your people telling you the truth? It isn't something they say in order to scare you into going back?"

Margaret, David, and Katherine all stared at me now. Then David smiled faintly.

"I'd almost forgotten we're in the bad old days," he said. "But we are. And although the bad old days have their compensations, it must be a great nuisance not knowing whether you can believe what you're told by the powers-that-be. John, the answer to your question is yes, we are sure. We believe we are told the truth."

Margaret and Katherine nodded in agreement.

"However," David went on, "I am going to bring my own grossly unfair form of persuasion to bear on Katherine. My dear, if you decide to stay, I shall stay as well. Not *with* you, you understand. I won't inflict my actual presence. But you'll know there are two of us in the condemned cell."

"David!" Margaret said.

"Oh, you couldn't, you couldn't!" That was Katherine. And now she was weeping.

"I think I shall go for a little walk," said Alan. He was embarrassed. "Nice scenery you have around here. I'll see you later."

"Perhaps I should go, too," I offered.

"No, John, please don't," Margaret said.

Terry Foster said, "David, it would be ridiculous for you to stay behind. It would just be the destruction of yourself as well as Katherine. And what about Margaret?"

"In that case," Margaret said, "I should stay also. My mission has been a fiasco anyway. If Katherine is determined, then we may as well all be written off."

"Listen," I said. "Couldn't something be done the other way round? Why don't you all go back to 2149 and take Ben with you?"

"You still haven't grasped the logic of time-change, John," said David kindly. "If we travel backward in time, we can return to our own day—or die, for that matter—and things can be restored as they were, with nothing changed. The fabric's not unraveled. But if a person went *forward* in time, then everything would be changed from now on and forever after. And that can't happen. You understand?"

"Well, sort of. I suppose so."

"I don't think you do entirely, do you, John?" said Margaret. "However, here's something you'll understand. Do you know why we all stared when we realized your brother was Benjamin Dunham?"

"No."

"Because Benjamin Dunham's a famous name to us. He's still remembered in our day. Like Fleming, or

Rutherford, or Watson and Crick. Two of the great names in twentieth-century science, for their work in low-temperature physics, are Dunham and Thompson. They always go together. I can't remember who Thompson was, or is, or will be . . .''

"*I* know who Thompson is,'' said Terry Foster quietly. He and Ben were both looking in Harold's direction. And Harold Thompson, in extreme embarrassment, blushed brightly.

"So you see, Ben,'' said David. "You can't shoot off into the future with your life's work undone. In that case it never *would* be done. A philosophical absurdity.''

"I don't deny it,'' said Ben. And then, slowly and painfully, "It seems that Katherine and I can have at most a few weeks together. At the cost of her life. And, if you carry out your threats, at the cost of your two lives as well.''

"They wouldn't!'' declared Katherine fiercely.

"Oh, yes, we would,'' David said. "Personally, I don't care all that much for my own time. Admittedly it's hygienic and civilized, and the disasters you people kept forecasting have never come about. I suppose common sense has prevailed. We haven't blown ourselves up, nobody's at war, nobody's hungry. We've balanced the birth and death rates, and we've got rid of alcohol and other dangerous drugs. The family unit's stronger than in your day. We still have names, not numbers, and they're much the same names as they always were. Believe it or not, there's still a King of England. We don't have automobiles—they were a transitional mode of transportation—but we can still take a punt along the Cambridge Backs. Above all, we have the rule of law and the rule of truth, and so long as we abide by them there's no unpleasantness. And yet . . . compared with the dirty, disreputable, colorful old twentieth century, I have to admit I find it dreary. I can give it up without a qualm. I shall have what fun I can before the bacteria get me.''

"It will be a rake's progress, I suspect," said Margaret. 'He will wallow in the past. And I shall look after him.''

"Katherine, my dear," Ben said. "There's only one answer. You must go with them, back to 2149.''

He put both arms round her. Tears ran down Katherine's cheeks.

"Do you realize you won't even remember me?'' she said. "By tomorrow you'll have forgotten everything. That's how it has to be. I shall remember *you* for the rest of my life, and I suppose the memory's better than nothing, but . . .''

"She's agreed to go back," Ben said. "And it's the right decision." He sounded desperate but resolved. "This is the last act. I knew it would be, really. I knew it as soon as we got here." He looked around him at the dim little attic. "It's the end of the world," he said. "The last place God made. It has the air of all refuges about it. A refuge of last resort.''

"Can't they have any more time at all together, Margaret?" Terry asked. "Not even a day or two?''

"We have to go tonight," Margaret said. "We've had one extension. There won't be another.''

"At least there's an hour or two for them to say good-bye," Terry Foster said. "I shall take the rest of you out to dinner. There must be somewhere in reach of here where one can eat. I'll charge it to expenses. The biggest story that ever came a journalist's way, and I shall never write a word of it."

He opened the door in the gable end. It was a fine summer evening now. The sky was still blue, but duskily gilt-edged. Golden globs of light floated on the canal, and a railway viaduct stood sharply black against the sun. David and Margaret, Terry and Harold went down the ladder. Alan was waiting below. I pulled the ladder up and took another look at the lovers before climbing down the crumbling brickwork. Ben and Katherine sat on the camp bed, silent, their arms still round each other. Katherine was weeping again, soundlessly. Ben kissed her cheeks, where the tears ran.

I would go on seeing Ben, but I wouldn't see Katherine again after tonight. I'd have liked to say something to her, but she was totally concentrated on him; there wasn't room in her mind for me. I left them alone.

twenty

It was an elaborate and long-drawn-out dinner at a downtown hotel—not the sort of thing I go for much, with a great display of white cloths and napkins, and foreign-accented waiters hovering around. But it did pass time, and that was what it was supposed to do. Everyone knew we didn't want to go back to that end-of-the-world attic on the canal bank until the final hour, though not a word was said. There wasn't in fact a great deal of conversation at all, and such as it was, it was mostly uneasy small talk. I was sitting next to Margaret and across the table from David, and I could almost see David's sense of responsibility returning as the time of departure drew near. When the waiter tried to refill his glass, he put a protective hand over it.

"There's something I'd like to know about," I said to Margaret. "The day before we went to the races, David went forward in time, didn't he, and looked up the results?"

"Yes, of course."

"He could have looked up all kinds of other things, couldn't he?" I said.

"Could and did," said David.

"Such as what's going to happen to my family," I said.

"Nothing easier," said David.

"John dear," said Margaret, "do you really want to know what's going to happen? If you thought about it, you might decide it's better not to."

"That sounds ominous," I said.

"Oh, not so," said David cheerfully, and then, "It doesn't matter how much we tell him, Margaret, it will all have gone from his mind in a couple of hours' time."

"I told you, David, I'm not so sure about John," Margaret said. "I think he may retain something—at least for a time. So be careful."

"Well, he realizes already that his brother's going to be a leading scientist. It can't do him any harm to know that his father and stepmother and he himself will all do well enough in the end, though not as brilliantly as Ben."

"Then Father will get the mastership?" I asked.

"Let's say that if I could place a bet on that, I wouldn't expect to lose my money," said David.

"The person I'm really thinking about," I said, "is Sarah. My sister. We worry a lot about Sarah."

"John!" said Margaret. "I tried to warn you . . ." She looked across the table at David.

David said brightly, "I predict for your sister a long, happy, healthy, successful life."

Margaret was silent, looking down at the tablecloth.

"One thing you've learned from us," I said to David bitterly, "is how to tell lies. But you haven't learned it very well."

*   *   *

211

There was still some light in the sky when we left the hotel. The doorman whistled up a taxi for us. Harold directed the driver, who hadn't heard of our destination. The journey took less than ten minutes, and when we reached the canal bank Ben and Katherine were waiting for us, dry-eyed and composed.

"We've said our good-bye," Ben told us.

"Good," said Margaret. "We must all do the same."

"I should like to watch you go, if I may," Terry said.

"You can all watch us go if you wish. But keep a little distance away. I don't want anybody misplaced in time, as Alan was when we arrived. There have been far too many hitches in this mission already. And it's too painful a parting to end with a muddle."

We were in the bare open space beside the row of cottages, with the canal on our right. Margaret clasped her hands together and seemed to be abstracted in thought for a minute. Then she said, "This place is all right for arrival. There's nothing built on it in our time. But we must stay in the open air. The building will go very soon, and that's dangerous."

There was a little round of farewells and embraces. I got a peck on the cheek from Katherine, a warm hug from Margaret, a cheerful handshake from David. Ben parted from Katherine in the end with no more than a pressure of the hand. He and Harold, Terry and Alan and I stood back, a few yards away from the visitors. Except for us, the area was deserted. David cast a look along the towpath in the direction of the battered old icebreaker. "I wish that could last long enough for me to get my hands on it again," he said ruefully.

"Well, this is it," Margaret said. "It may take us two or

212

three tries to get into synchronization, but when we do, we shall go quickly.''

She and Katherine and David clasped one another, putting their heads together as if sharing some profound secret, though no word was said. The silence became oppressive, and you could sense an agony of concentration. And then the dizziness came. The dingy brick building behind the visitors, the railway viaduct, the canal, and the high walls of factories at the other side of it were spinning, spinning. Slowly they came to a halt and were steady again. Then there was a shattering of the air, as if an enormous sheet of invisible glass had broken. The visitors were still clasped together.

Behind them the old brick building suddenly collapsed. One instant it was there, the next it wasn't; there was just a pile of rubble on the ground. A brief tremble, and the canal bank was all grass and trees. Then came a voice—the crisp feminine voice I'd heard at Cambridge in that moment when the visitors arrived.

"No! No!'' it ordered. "Back a bit!''

The trees and grass vanished, and the building flew together again. It looked newer, less dilapidated than before. The name of the canal company was painted on its side in large letters.

"Too far!'' the voice said wearily. "Forward a bit, slowly. Katherine, concentrate! Do you hear me? Concentrate!''

Another shiver, as of the invisible glass. The building was shabbier, and nameless again. An iron staircase led down from that midair door in its gable end. A small, very old man in a neat blue suit was walking down it. But with another brief shudder the old man was gone, and the

213

staircase too. A small child with fair curly hair, wearing a short shabby dress, stood in the open doorway.

"Jean!" said Harold Thompson. "My sister Jean! The spitting image of her, when she was little. We lived here for a while, fifteen years ago. This is like revisiting old times!"

"Exactly!" I said.

The visitors didn't seem to see or hear anything. They were huddled together, still fiercely intent.

"Again!" said the crisp feminine voice. A tremble in the air and the child was gone, the door closed, the whole place a little more dilapidated than before. Across the open space toward the building walked a small thin man wearing a black beret and carrying a tiny suitcase. A strange, bitter-looking man; a man who unaccountably made my flesh creep. But before he reached the building he was shuddered away and a couple was standing there, looking up speculatively at that same door. A tall thin boy of about my age and a plump blond girl, arms twined round each other's waists.

"Will you please *concentrate*, Katherine!" ordered the clear authoritative voice. "CONCENTRATE!" And then the figures of boy and girl had gone, the air seemed to stabilize, and everything looked normal. But the tiny circle made by the visitors had expanded, and in the middle of them was a fourth person, whom I couldn't see clearly.

"Sonia!" said Margaret.

"We're in phase at last!" said the voice. "And high time, too! All right. Quickly, before we lose it. Katherine, you must *not* look round. Now, off we go!"

From our group, somebody called a good-bye, but the

visitors, huddling together, took no notice. For a few seconds they stood there, intensely concentrated in themselves, excluding all around them. And then they were gone, so suddenly that I felt as if I'd blinked them away. Where they had been, there remained for an instant a curious gap, a kind of hole in the air; but it mended at once and there was nothing to see but the shabby, ordinary old building.

I looked round at the four remaining people: Terry, Harold, Alan, and Ben. On Ben's face was such pain as I'd never seen there before. Terry's expression was one of fascinated interest; the others showed only astonishment. And as I watched, the expressions changed, became blank, as if something were fading from all four minds. I tried to speak to them; my lips framed words but I didn't hear anything come out, and nobody seemed to hear me. In another instant they too had vanished, and I was alone.

And back came the dizziness, more overpowering than ever. The aged building looped the loop, stood still for a moment, then turned over again and began to spin, faster and faster, disappearing into a dizzy circle; and then my surroundings had gone altogether and it was I myself who was spinning, spinning in a vortex. From somewhere the word "Restore!" came into my mind. And I was sucked into the heart of the whirlpool, and all went black.

Coming out of blackness, as if out of sleep in a totally dark room, I felt self-enclosed at first. Then I was aware that there was a world outside myself, but I didn't know where I was. The blackness faded to dusk, and there was sky above, and I realized I was out of doors. My surroundings resolved themselves and became familiar. Trees, grass, a river, and in the foreground a weathered teak table. Our garden. And the garden had people in it. Father was sitting at the teak table, Ben sprawled beside me on the grass, and next to him was Sarah, sitting with hands clasped round her knees. My first conscious thought was that she should have been in bed long ago.

"And so," Father was saying, "there's more to be said for old-fashioned ways of teaching this subject than is sometimes admitted . . . Ben! What was that?"

"You jumped."

"So did you."

"Why? What happened?"

"I don't think anything happened," said Father. "But yes, I jumped. A funny feeling. The kind you get sometimes if you're on the point of going to sleep and you suddenly jerk yourself awake. I suppose that's what it was. My own eloquence sending me to sleep. Strange. I've often been made sleepy by other people's eloquence, but never before by my own . . ."

"It felt like something more than that to me," said Ben.

"Yes, you look rather shaken," said Father. "As if you'd seen a ghost, as the saying goes."

"I feel a bit as if I'd seen a ghost," said Ben. "Or had some kind of spooky experience, I don't know what."

And suddenly it dawned on me. Restoration had taken place. The visitors, or the people in charge of their project, had put everything back as if nothing had happened. The reason why Ben and I weren't on the bank of that northern canal anymore was because to all intents and purposes we never *had* been there. We were now doing what we'd have been doing at this moment if the strangers had never come to Cambridge.

216

All that remained was my own recollection. Did I share it with Ben, or had he forgotten already? It rather looked as if he had.

"It's odd that we should both jump like that at the same moment," Father was saying. But he wasn't really very interested. This might have been any summer evening in our garden, with nothing to make it special.

The discussion on teaching methods went on, but was rather one-sided. Ben wasn't contributing anything, just staring into space in a puzzled way. Eventually Father got up and went into the house. Ben and I were still sitting on the grass, and Sarah, unnoticed, was at the teak table.

I thought I'd better test Ben. "Did you feel dizzy a moment ago?" I asked him.

"Yes, I did, actually," said Ben, surprised.

"Like Alan the other week, when we first met the Wyatts."

"Wyatts? Who are they? I don't know any Wyatts." And then, slowly, "The name seems to ring a bell, though. John, there's something that's bothering me, just beyond the edge of my mind. It's as if I'd had an extraordinary dream that I couldn't quite recall. There was a boat. Harold Thompson's boat. And a building on a canal bank. And a girl. Oh, yes, there was a girl . . . It doesn't feel like a dream, though. It feels kind of real but fading."

He frowned. He was groping for it, groping without success. A minute later he shook his head. "Dizziness, hallucinations . . . It must be old age. Or overwork."

"It couldn't be overwork," I said. And there was a bit of ribbing between us. Ben said nothing more about any unusual experience. I decided that if he hadn't forgotten

217

already, he soon would have. I was fairly sure I would forget as well, but obviously nothing like so soon. At that moment it was all clear and exact in my mind. A pity, I felt, that it would be lost. But there, the fabric had been restored, as it had to be. The images in my mind were all that was left. They would go, and then there'd be nothing.

And then the thought occurred to me. While I still remembered, I could write it all down. Then it wouldn't be lost. As restoration had taken place already, it couldn't affect what I was going to write now. I could do it during the summer vacation, if I got a move on. It would be a race against time.

It's fading now, as I pen this final paragraph. It's been fading slowly for quite a while. But I've finished my account. I've got it all down. I've won.

twenty-one,

Well that's it, just as I found it. As I said at the start, I can hardly remember putting it on paper, though the paper is there all right and sometimes I feel that my writing hand remembers the effort. Perhaps I too have had my Xanadu.

Is the story true? For quite a while I had my doubts. There's obviously a sense in which nothing happened, whichever way you look at it. Mrs. McGuinness says she never managed to rent her rooms again after the students left. Her mirror is all in one piece. The name of Wyatt means nothing to her or to Father. Nobody suggests that Ben ever disappeared from home, and Alan Stubbings seems unaware of any encounter on the Backs. Yet after all, if you accept what was said about restoration, these things are to be expected and don't disprove the narrative at all.

What inclines me to believe it is that Ben, though he could remember so little, behaved for a long time as if he'd suffered some great though inexplicable loss. In fact Ben has never been quite the same as he used to be. Laura remarked on the change in him, only the other week.

"You know," she said, "there's a big difference in Ben these days. He used to be so boyish about anything that wasn't connected with his work. You'd think he'd never worried, never suffered, didn't even know there was such a thing as suffering, except maybe as a piece of abstract information. Now I feel there's more depth to him. He's growing up emotionally."

"About time, too," my father said.

"Some of us," said Laura dryly, "never manage it at all."

The other thing that inclines me toward belief is a tiny incident when Ben and I were chatting in the kitchen one evening at dusk. Sarah was there, but as so often she was quiet and inconspicuous, and we'd practically forgotten her presence. I'd been reading through the manuscript earlier that day, for the third or fourth time, and it suddenly occurred to me to ask Ben if he knew a girl at Bristol called Elaine. Ben seemed mildly surprised, and said he did.

"She's quite a bright girl," he said. "Sometimes I think she rather fancies me. She's the serious type, though. If she gets going with a man, she'll want it to be for years if not forever. Now as for me, all things considered, I think I'm a born bachelor."

"You don't have a dream girl, Ben?" I asked him.

"I don't go in for dreams much," he said. But this reminded him of something and he grew thoughtful.

"Yes," he said. "Perhaps I do have a dream girl. She's dark and tall and strange, and however long I know her I won't know anything about her, not really, whereas I know all I want to know about Elaine, and maybe more . . . This is a silly conversation, John. One doesn't actually meet one's dream girl. Dream girls are kid stuff. One shouldn't *have* such a thing."

"You might have met her already," I said.

"That's an odd thought," said Ben. "Curiously enough, I sometimes feel that myself. As if I've known and lost and forgotten her. But as if she's around somewhere all the time, remembering me. And I think of the dream I told you about, if it *was* a dream, in the garden that evening. All I remember now is that it was very vivid and very unhappy. Or maybe it was very happy. That's funny, isn't it, John? I really don't know which."

Sarah's voice, composed and reassuring, came out of the half-light.

"It was happy, Ben."

Ben stared at her, then laughed indulgently.

"What do *you* know about my dreams?" he said.

"Sarah knows a lot," I told him. And as she turned toward me I looked into her wide gray eyes and knew she knew more than I'd realized.

"You remember, don't you, minnow?" I asked her quietly.

"Yes, John," she said.

About the Author

John Rowe Townsend's novels for young readers have been widely acclaimed. *Noah's Castle,* published in 1976, was chosen as a notable book by the American Library Association, and was also on the ALA list of best books for young adults. This was Mr. Townsend's seventh appearance on ALA lists.

In addition, *The Intruder,* an honors-list book for the Carnegie Medal in 1969, won the 1970 Boston Globe–Horn Book award for excellence of text, an Edgar from the Mystery Writers of America, and a Silver Pen from the English Center of International PEN. *Hell's Edge* was a runner-up for the Carnegie Medal in 1963.

Mr. Townsend lives in Cambridge, England, where *The Visitors* is set. A recognized authority on children's literature, he is the author of two books on the subject, *Written for Children* and *A Sense of Story.*